Candid Camera

By

HA Blackwood

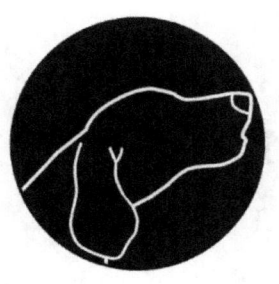

Baying Hound's Dark Side

USA

Disclaimers and Copyright

Candid Camera

Acknowledgments

I want to extend a special thanks to Chaturbate models Anna Haven and Ivy Ward. I started out researching the cam industry and exhausted what the internet 'how to' guides could tell me, so I had to dive in and actually use the site. Other sites offer streaming cams, but Chaturbate is currently the largest and most used site, so that's where I went. I had an idea what I would find there, and to some extent, I was right. There's a lot of sex, much of it graphic and very, very explicit. I read a blog post once—sadly, I can't remember the author—that had a great line in it: don't yuck someone else's yum. So, while I try not to pass judgment, much of what I initially found on Chaturbate just wasn't for me.

However, I hit the jackpot my first night on the site and lucked into Anna's room. Anna was charming, beautiful, sweet, kind, gracious, humble, and genuine. She's fluent in two languages (English and Hungarian), and her very slight accent is one aspect of her sexy charm.

Yes, I know she's running a business, and yes, I know her job is to get people to stay in her chat room and hand over money. That's how every business works. The trick to this particular business is making people do so gladly and then return a couple nights later to do it again. With Anna, people do just that. Both men and women watch her shows and tip generously. Anna's gift is that she makes people *want* to do it. It feels *good* to hit that tip button, and she does it without obvious trickery or guilt. In other words, she's good at her job.

Ivy Ward visited one of Anna's shows, and Anna recommended that we follow her. Ivy is much more casual in her room. She's charming and funny (she laughs a *lot*), and what she can do with her clothes *on* is enough to get your blood pumping. And not for nothing, but that woman has *moves*. If you've never seen someone dance while kneeling on a bed, it's way sexier than you can imagine without seeing it.

Ivy was also kind enough to spend some time with me outside the Chaturbate environment, answering my many questions about the *other* side of the chat screen. Her input has hopefully helped make this a more realistic representation of this fantastic virtual economy. If, after reading, you found it believable, she gets the credit. If not, I take the blame.

Anna and Ivy – I want to say a big thanks to both of you ladies for showing me that the cam industry is more than watching group sex and octopus tentacle dildo demonstrations (not that there's anything wrong with those). Yes, at its core, it's about sex and money. But it's also about building relationships, sharing time, providing support, and building a community. I learned a lot from both of you, and bits and pieces found their way into the fictitious world of Candid Camera. I hope I represent your business fairly and honestly. Mostly, I hope this book does well because I need to buy more tokens.

-    HA Blackwood

One

I absently caressed Gemma's arm while I lay on the couch with my head in her lap. We had a mutual affection for *The Fifth Element*, specifically for Mila Jovovich, so I had it streaming on VUDU. Gemma was buried in her phone. I paused the movie and rolled over so I could peer up at her. Her beautiful brown eyes darted back and forth as she scrolled through her email.

I pulled my shirt up, exposing my breasts, and ran my fingernails over them, bringing my pink nipples to attention.

"I see that," Gemma said without taking her eyes off her phone. She switched it to her left hand and started feeling me up with her right.

I was just trying to get her attention, but her touch felt lovely. I scooted a little closer, edging my shoulders onto her leg, and lay on my back, giving her better access to my chesticles. She obliged by tickling me with her fingertips from my navel to my collarbones. I closed my eyes and just enjoyed it for a moment.

Gemma and I had been dating for several weeks when she made a significant decision. "I'm expanding the house," she said one night over her famous Caprese chicken.

"Expanding? Why?"

"There's not enough room for you."

We often spent the night at each other's house, seldom going more than one night alone in a bed. But during the day, there wasn't enough space in her house for me to work, and while my house had an extra bedroom she could use for an office, it didn't have her glorious bathroom or kitchen. Plus, she had the neighborhood pool that we frequently used, even sneaking in to skinny dip a few nights over those first few weeks together. We weren't ready to move in together, but we didn't really want to be apart either.

"Gemma, you don't need to do anything crazy like that, especially not for me!"

"Well, I hate that we have to split up every day because I don't have a big enough office for us both."

"We'd have to do that anyway if one of us didn't work from home."

"But we do work from home. And if you stay over, it seems kind of dumb for you to go back to your house to work."

"Well, if I have an office here, there's really no reason for me to ever leave. It would be like me moving in."

She smiled. "What's wrong with that idea?"

This took me by surprise. We were both independent, self-sufficient, and irresistibly drawn to each other. But I liked owning my own place. I liked that I had that equity in my pocket, so to speak. And I didn't like the idea of Gemma spending a lot of money on me, when who knew what the future would bring? I mean, sure, we were happy *now*, but neither of us had what you would call a stellar track record with relationships. Of course, I'd never been happier than I was with Gemma, and I knew she felt the same way. Still, I was concerned about Gemma taking on the expense of this move.

It was as if she was reading my mind. "I've already talked to a contractor and gotten a bid. I'll take out a line of credit to cover the remodel. You can either sell or rent your place. I'd refinance the house and put you on the mortgage. So, either way, you still own a house."

"Are you asking me to marry you?"

She laughed. "What? No! Let's take that way slow, sister. On the mortgage, we'll be tenants in common. Co-owners."

I let it ruminate for a minute. "How soon do you want to do this?"

"They can start next week if I can come stay at your place."

"What about all your stuff?"

3

"I'll have movers bring the essentials over to your house, and the rest they'll put in PODs on my driveway." She took a pull from her glass of wine. "What do you say? Will you be my live-in lover?"

I looked around. It was a really nice house; it was just small. But could I do it? Just a few minutes ago, we weren't ready to live together, and now we were going to own property jointly?

I thought about the alternative. We would never be able to both work at home in her house as it was now, and with her amenities, this was the nicer place to be. And she did have a huge yard, so she had room to expand.

And why wouldn't I want to live with her? On the one hand, I'd had nothing but a string of dead-end relationships, with both men and women, for the last ten years—ever since Gemma took my lesbian virginity in the basement of a frat house my sophomore year of college. After a decade of longing to find her again, we were reunited, and neither of us had been happier in our lives. This just felt like such a big step. We were both just over thirty. Had we even finished sowing our oats?

But, it was the natural progression of things, right? I mean, if we continued to have to split time between houses like this, how long would it be before one of us wouldn't feel like driving the fifteen minutes to the other's house one night, and we'd stay apart. One night would eventually become two, and we'd drift apart. If I wanted this relationship to flourish, we needed to go to the next level. Right?

"Okay," I agreed. "Let's do it."

We clinked our glasses, finished dinner, and ripped each other's clothes off. Later, as we lay entwined on her bed, slick with each other's juices, she fell asleep with her head on my chest. I brushed her raven-black curls away from her face and watched her eyes twitching behind their lids. The feel of her body pressed against mine, her rhythmic breathing, the musky smell of our sex... yeah, I wanted this forever.

Smash cut to three weeks later, and there I was, tits up, laying in her lap on my couch, getting stroked like a cat, and she couldn't tear herself away from her phone.

"Are we going to watch this movie, or what?"

She didn't look up. Yet again. "Turn it back on if you want."

I sat up, frustrated. "What do you mean *if I want*? I thought *you* wanted to watch it too! But you won't put your phone down!"

Gemma finally looked up at me. My anger faded as I saw a look on her face that I'd only seen once before, when she told me that she used to be a stripper slash escort slash prostitute, and on the night she fucked me in that frat house basement, she'd been paid to do so.

She was afraid then, and she was afraid now. "What? Gemma, what is it?"

"I have another secret to tell you."

TWO

"It must be a doozie of a secret to put that expression on your face. Is this a 'we shouldn't have decided to build a house together' kind of secret?"

Her face remained stone serious. "I hope to god not. I really do."

I pulled my shirt down, covering my breasts, and leaned back against the opposite end of the couch. "That wasn't a no, which is what I was expecting you to say. Well, get it out."

She looked back at her phone, deciding how to start. "I just heard from an old friend in LA. She needs my help with something related to finances, and I really need to be there for her."

"Okay...so what's the secret? Is she an old flame?"

"Not exactly, though full disclosure, she and I fucked. A lot. But it was for work. Darcy, I told you that I had stories that rivaled yours. Well, this is a big part of it. I was sort of a porn star for several years when I was in LA."

I thought about the video that my last girlfriend and her husband made of the three of us fucking, and how nonplussed Gemma had been by it. In fact, she acted impressed by the number of views and ratings it had. Her laissez-faire attitude made more sense in this context. But—*porn star?* "Are we talking like, Jenna Jameson type porn star, or what? You have to elaborate, please."

She sighed. "Okay, it was amateur porn, kind of. The first thing you have to understand, a lot of amateur porn isn't really amateur. It's not scripted, exactly, but the scenarios are set up in advance."

"You mean a middle-aged man doesn't really drive a cab around London and happen to pick up dozens of random, horny women who want his enormous cock in their asses? Color me shocked."

"Well, yeah. I mean, the intent is to make people think it's just random, but on some level, everyone knows it's not. But if you do it right, that line is blurred. You think it's not real, but...."

"Right, like the guy who commented on my video that he thought I was a good actress because I looked like I was being slut-shamed by Kim and Pete, but he knew it was really scripted. Except it wasn't."

Gemma nodded. "Except it was. You just weren't in on it. Kim and Pete had a plan, and you went for it all the way. The three of you were hot as shit, with real orgasms, and the part where they threw you out was where people assumed it was scripted. Because it was. See, the line was blurred, it was hot as shit, and that's why it was rated over ninety percent with two hundred fifty-thousand views."

"I thought it was one hundred thousand?"

"It's gone up over the last few weeks. I told you, it's hot."

"You've been watching it!"

She blushed, then shrugged. "When I don't have you here, I can at least masturbate to you. Maybe a couple hundred of those views are me."

"Okay, thanks for the master's class in amateur porn directing. So you need to go on a trip to see an old flame who desperately needs your help? Does it get worse than that?"

"Well, she's in town. She wants to meet."

"I see. Tonight?"

"I told her it has to wait until tomorrow. But yeah, she wants to meet ASAP."

I nodded absently. "Okay. Let's meet her."

Gemma blinked in surprise. "You don't need to get involved with this. She can wait."

"How many times did you console me by saying *your past is part of who you are. It's what brought you here?* Well, the same goes for you. We're moving in together, Gemma. You're having your house remodeled to fit me into your life. So, I'm in. Where you go, I go."

"I'm not planning on fucking her if that's what you're thinking."

"Well, maybe I am. We can be Eskimo Sisters."

Gemma chuckled at that, her serious face melting into a smile. "You really want to do this now?"

"Yes." I bounced on the couch and caught Gemma watching my tits bound around under my shirt. "I'm excited to meet your porno lover!"

"Okay." Gemma gave me a disapproving look but started texting. "I'll set it up."

Three

I turned the movie back on while Gemma waited for her friend to respond to her. It was another Mila Jovovich movie, only this time it was *Resident Evil*. Mila and Michelle Rodriguez! Score!

After a couple of back-and-forth messages, she looked over at me.

"So... you want to be slutty tonight?"

I did, and I didn't. "It depends what you have in mind."

"Ashleigh wants to meet at Poppa Chubby's."

"The strip club."

"Yes."

I'd never been there, but I'd heard that it was wild. Guys could get laid there if they played their cards right. And, oh yeah, Gemma used to work there! "Yes, let's do it. But you have to tell me some of this story while we get ready. I wish I'd known we were going to do this. I'd have gotten a wax yesterday."

"I love your fuzzy beaver." She caught my eye roll. "I'm serious! Your red hair is a complete fucking turn-on!"

"Good, because I'm not shaving it. I get too itchy."

"I'll scratch your itch." She reached over and put her hand in my pants and gave me a few playful scratches as we walked to the master bedroom.

"Keep that up, and we're not leaving the house tonight."

She laughed and withdrew her hand. She had her shirt off, then slipped her shorts and panties down in one motion, depositing them all in the hamper. I stared at her body as she reached into the shower to turn the water on.

I ditched my clothes and turned back to the shower, where Gemma tested the water temperature with an extended foot. Her dark Italian skin stood out against the white tile of the shower wall. The soft curls of her raven-black hair fell between her shoulders, and her toned legs led all the way up to her round ass. She turned toward me, giving me a good look at her firm breasts with hard, brown nipples in the center. A ridge of muscles was just visible on her abdomen, gradually narrowing in a V to just above her pubic mound. Below, her beautifully bald vagina beckoned me to come closer.

We'd measured each other to get a feel for how well we could wear each other's clothes. Really it was just foreplay, an excuse to play with each other's bodies. Gemma's figure measured 37-28-38, while mine was 39-28-36, making me a little more top-heavy than her, and she hippier than me, but for the most part, we could wear all but each other's most form-fitting clothes.

I walked over to her and grabbed her head, pulling her close to me, and kissed her. I didn't start slow and gentle; I stormed her lips and invaded her mouth with my tongue. Her initial resistance vanished, and she wrapped her arms around me, her tongue mounting a spirited defense of its territory. She lifted a leg, forcing me to slide my feet farther apart, and she rubbed her thigh against my pussy. My desire to go to Poppa Chubby's was disappearing, and my desire to devour my lover was taking its place.

She broke off the kiss. "You're killing me, Darcy. God, I want you so bad. You're getting ravished later tonight."

I smiled as she turned and stepped into the shower. I couldn't believe that I was hers and she was mine. As I watched the water cascade through her hair and down her body, a line from the Fifth Element popped into my head. *She's perfect.*

I stepped in behind her and pulled the door closed. I was looking forward to the time when we would move back into Gemma's place and could use her massive shower again. Mine was too cramped.

We traded positions while she lathered her hair. I got mine wet and gave the shampoo bottle a couple of pumps.

"Okay, Gemma, give me some background on what I'm in for tonight."

She grabbed the soap and rubbed it all over my body. God, I loved showering with her. "Okay. I told you I was a stripper at the club, and I was paid to come to the party where we met. And I also told you that I did some gay-for-pay action at the club, right?"

"Yeah, you told me that."

"Well, Ashleigh was my partner for those shenanigans."

"Wait, I thought she was your friend from LA?"

"She is. Or was. She worked here, then there, and now she's back here. I'll explain it to you. After that night with you, I told you I was upset that my job would keep us apart. I just knew that if you found out I was paid to fuck you, you'd hate me, and I couldn't face that. I wanted to hang onto that one perfect night, the night where I fell for you. So, I quit, and I was going to make something of myself, so I'd never have to make that choice again."

Four

Gemma's Story
Ten Years Ago

"Gemma, there's a kid out here, wants to meet you."

She turned and looked at Andre, the big black bouncer Chubby hired to guard the dressing room and keep the girls safe from the creeps. Andre was a genuinely nice guy who watched out for the girls like they were his sisters. He even turned down sex when it had been offered by some of the girls. He had a standard response: "I start fucking you girls, and I'll let my guard down. Someone's gonna get hurt then, and Andre's gonna be looking for a new job. And Andre's got mouths to feed, you feel me? Thank you, though, baby-girl." Andre called all the dancers 'baby-girl.'

Gemma sighed. "Okay. Stay close, though, okay?"

"I'll be your shadow, baby-girl."

She walked out the door to the left of the stages and found a clean-cut guy waiting with his hands in his pockets. She recognized him from earlier in the night when she and Ashleigh had eaten each other out doing their 'gay for pay' act on stage.

"Hey, uh, Alexis? I think that's what they called you... that's your stage name, right? I'm Boomer."

"Hi, Boomer. What do you want?" She wasn't in the mood for small talk.

"I was just wondering, um, for this girl-on-girl show, um how much would it cost to get you to come to my frat and do it with a girl we pick out?"

Gemma's red-flag alert went up. "What for? Why don't you come here and watch it for free? Or do you have a girl picked out already?"

"Does it matter why? I mean, we'd be paying you...."

"Of course it matters, Boomer. The reason always matters. Why pay me for something you can get for a cover charge here? I'm losing interest...."

"It's an initiation thing for our freshman pledges. They have to masturbate, and they get different house assignments and duties based on the order they finish."

It was creepy, juvenile frat-boy antics, but they *were* juvenile frat boys. Besides, she'd fucked guys at the club for as little as fifty bucks when she was desperate for cash. Her usual rate was five hundred for an out-call. She looked Boomer in the eyes. "Two thousand."

His mouth dropped open. "That much? Holy shit, that's a lot of money! I can go... fifteen hundred."

Gemma hid her glee, faking like she was doing some mental math. "I suppose I can do it for fifteen. When?"

"Next Friday night."

"Oh, kid," she said, though he was probably two years older than her. "We're back to two grand. Friday's my biggest moneymaker."

"Well, what if we do it later? Like eleven?"

She noodled on it for a minute. She could work the after-dinner crowd, five to nine, go home, shower, and hit their frat house by eleven. "Okay, deal. Half now."

Boomer grimaced and pulled out his wallet, withdrawing a stack of hundred-dollar bills. He counted off eight and handed them over. Gemma folded the bills and put them in her back pocket. "What's the address?"

"Um, you owe me fifty bucks back."

"I'm not a fucking change machine, kid, unless you want singles. The address?"

"Wait, how do I know you'll show up?"

"You think I'm going to take your eight hundred bucks and retire to an island or something? I'll show up because I want another seven hundred.

Or I can give you your money back, and you find someone else for your little lesbo fuck party."

"No, no, this works." He wrote the address on a slip of paper and handed it to her. "Thanks, uh..."

"Alexis," Gemma said.

"Don't I get to know your real name?"

"Not while you're paying me. See you Friday." She turned and went back to the dressing room, Andre in tow.

"You want some muscle at that party, baby-girl?"

"Aren't you working?"

"I got some brothers that would do it. Shit, they'd probably do it for free if they got to watch the show."

She smiled. "No, I'll be okay. I feel bad for whatever poor girl they get to go along with it. She's going to get it from me, and good!"

"Well, you let me know if you change your mind. I'm not real comfortable with you going there alone."

"I will. Thanks, big bro."

"Any time, baby girl."

The big man lumbered off.

A week later, Gemma sat in front of her mirror, thinking about the frat house party the night before. The girl the Sigma Omega guys had hired her to fuck was still tattooed on the inside of her eyelids. Even though she had performed the girl-on-girl act on stage a bunch of times, it had never made Gemma cum. She was always painfully aware of the audience, of the screams and whistles, of the singles, fives, tens, and the occasional twenty that were thrown at them. Ashleigh, or Mercedes, as she was known on stage, had her close a few times, but she never tipped over the edge, and the big climax was always a fake.

That red-haired woman the night before was something special, though. Part of it, Gemma assumed, was psychological. The woman wasn't being paid to do an act like they were at the club.

When one of the guys announced he had a woman willing to do it—"She's GTG," he shouted, meaning she was *good to go,* Gemma was shocked, but she went for it. This woman had never been with a woman before, and she gave herself over to Gemma completely. That was a huge factor for Gemma—this was *real.* And in return, she changed Gemma's world.

As the woman went down on her, Gemma didn't see a coworker. She saw a lusty redhead eager to eat her pussy. Those bright eyes looking up at her, making eye contact, asking silently if she was doing it

19

right, sent thrills through her body, and the room full of frat boys faded into the background. Even the bukkake game the freshmen were forcing each other to play barely registered with her. Gemma was consumed by that beautiful face and the earnest way the woman wanted to please her. When the guys started running a train on the girl, she never lost focus, determined to make Gemma explode. And explode she did. She'd never cum with such physical or emotional force before.

Later in the night, she and the girl were in the midst of a threesome. One of the frat boys, a kid named Peter, had escorted them from the basement, protecting them from a crowd of drunk, horny boys, and this was Gemma's way of repaying the favor. Peter was eating the girl out, and Gemma was riding her face, wanting to see if she could make her cum again.

Gemma could not believe how good this beginner was at bringing her pleasure. She had never considered herself bisexual because the lesbian act at the club was just that; an act. But while she face-fucked this neophyte, Gemma could imagine dating her. She would swear off men if this woman asked her to. By the time she came, Gemma wanted nothing more than to curl up next to the girl, hold her tight, and sleep the rest of the night with their bodies pressed together. But she knew as soon as the woman found out the truth—that she, Gemma, had been paid to fuck her—the woman was sure to hate her. College-educated women did not go for strip club trash like Gemma Amante or 'Alexis' as she was known on stage. So, Gemma told Peter to fuck the girl, and the girl, for her part, happily accepted his cock.

Peter had washed their clothes and put them in the dryer, so Gemma snuck off and retrieved them. She was getting dressed, and as she was pulling on her G-string, she looked at the woman's white panties with the red heart on them. Gemma slid the G-string off and folded the strings behind the swatch of fabric that barely was enough to cover her labia and sat it on the girl's clothes. She slipped the white panties on and slinked out of the room as the frat boy was pounding the girl from behind. While she'd never see her again, at least Gemma had that heart to remember her by.

"Are you okay?"

Gemma looked over at Ashleigh. She was the only dancer at the club that was nice to Gemma. Since they'd eaten each other out on stage several times, that made them about as close as two people could be. "No, not really. I can't do this anymore. I want a regular relationship. I want to be in love."

Ashleigh smiled. "What's his name, and where did you meet him?"

"I didn't get her name," Gemma said. It felt freeing to say *her* out loud. "It was a gay-for-pay gig last night. And she was incredible."

"Oh, honey, you can't fall for a client! You know that. It never works out, except in the movies."

"She wasn't the client. It was at a frat party, and she had no idea why I was there. She gave herself to me, and I gave myself to her. It was beautiful. But I know that when she found out I was paid to be there, she'd hate me."

"So, don't tell her. That's an easy fix."

"Right. How long before one of the frat guys let it slip? They probably already told her. God, I can't go out there tonight."

"Girl, you need a vacation. Go to LA. Get some beach time. I'll talk to Jade, we'll cover your stage time. I could use the extra cash anyway."

Gemma took her advice. She packed up the little bit of stuff at her makeup station and left out the back door. Three days later, she was in Los Angeles.

She had enough money for about two weeks in a hotel. Two weeks to find a job and a path to a better life. She realized pretty quickly that she didn't have the skills she'd need to make the leap to a legitimate, respectable job—the kind someone like that red-headed college girl would accept—and the recession made it worse. Any job she was qualified for had hundreds of applicants. People with master's degrees were taking entry-level positions. With her cash reserve almost gone, she was about to give up and return home, but she wasn't the type of girl to quit that easily. She did have one skill set that the overeducated briefcase crowd didn't.

She was rejected from the third strip club when she was approached in the parking lot by a voluptuous Hispanic woman as she walked to her car.

"Hold up a minute, girl. I heard the manager give you shade back there. You looking for work?"

Gemma was one step shy of desperate. "Yes."

"You have experience stripping?"

"Yes."

"Are you averse to being filmed having sex?"

Gemma opened her mouth to say thanks, but no thanks, but the woman cut her off.

"Before you turn me down, it's not your typical porn work. I mean, some of it is, but it's more than that. My girlfriend and I, we're starting something different. It's kind of a *for* girls, *by* girls thing." She fished a fifty-dollar bill from her pocket and held it out to Gemma. "I can see you're hesitant. Look, I'm just scouting for talent here, and I really like your look. I think you'd do well with us. There's an address on that bill. Come over tomorrow and talk to my girl. She's the business-minded one."

"What's your name?"

"Oh, my bad, where are my manners. I'm Reesie. Reesie Love. Well, Lovato, but I use Love professionally. What's yours?"

"Gemma Amante."

"Alright, Gemma. I hope to see you tomorrow. If not, keep the fifty. Nothing ventured, nothing gained, right? If I'm not there, ask for Tawney."

Back at the motel, Gemma found the manager waiting for her when she pulled into the lot.

"You're late on rent, girlie."

"I can't be, Mark. I paid a week in advance."

"That was last Friday. Now it's *this* Friday, and you owe me money. Either four-fifty for the week or seventy-five for the night."

All she had was the fifty Reesie had given her and a couple hundred in the bank, and she'd need that for gas to get home if the meeting the following day didn't pan out. "Can I pay you tomorrow?"

"Sure, you can pay me tomorrow for tomorrow's rent. You can pay me tonight for tonight's rent."

"What if I give you today and tomorrow's rent, plus ten percent for letting me float a day."

"I do that for you, every low life and grifter in this place is gonna want the same treatment, and I ain't going down that road." He looked her up and down, absently adjusting his penis in his pants. "Ass, grass or cash, babe. No one rides for free."

"You can't be serious."

"How's this for serious? Give me the money or get your shit and get out. What's it gonna be?"

She debated just getting her stuff and sleeping in her car, but she wanted to shower and look good for her meeting.

"What's it gonna be, dollface? Decision time."

Gemma sighed and started toward her room. "Fuck. Let's go."

The next day Gemma showed up at a house in the Hollywood Hills. The driveway was gated, and she pressed the intercom button. After a few seconds, a woman's voice said, "Yeah?"

"I'm Gemma Amante. Reesie asked me to come here today. If she's not here, she said I should ask for Tawney."

The gate buzzed and started rolling to the side. Gemma let it clear the entry before she pulled

25

through. The long drive ended at an expansive courtyard with a huge garage on the left. Several cars were backed against it, parked at an angle. She was surprised that most of them were as modest as her Volkswagen Jetta.

To the right was a massive house. It was the size of her apartment building back home. The front door opened, and Reesie walked out. She wore a white bando bikini top, a maroon string bottom, and sandals. An animal print scarf was tied over the top of her head Bettie Page-style, holding her lengthy, black hair out of her face. "Hi, Gemma! I'm so glad you came! Tawney and I were just talking about you! Come on in!"

Gemma had seen the big rose tattoo on Reesie's right hand last night, but her shirt had covered the devil's head in the middle of her forearm and the butterfly by her elbow. A sugar skull with roses growing from its eye sockets adorned her upper arm. Four inches below her navel, just above the bikini brief, she had a tattoo that read *Breathe Deep* on one line, and underneath it *and greet your doom*. Across her chest, above the bando top, she had a pair of swallows with *Just For Luck* strung between them as if they were holding a banner.

Gemma guessed that Reesie's measurements were 34-26-40. Her wide hips and ample ass swayed hypnotically as she led Gemma into the house.

Gemma found it interesting that there were no tattoos on her back, legs, or buttocks. Gemma didn't have any tattoos, nor did she want one, but for some reason, she found Reesie to be very sexy with them. Dressed in her shorts and short-sleeved blouse, she also felt surprisingly over-dressed.

She looked around as they passed through the entry. A staircase to the right led up to a long balcony that looked down on the entrance and a huge living room bigger than Gemma's entire apartment back home.

Reesie led her down the hall, through the massive kitchen, and out onto a large deck. Gemma looked around. This deck was also larger than her apartment. Several women were laying on chaise lounges or on towels, catching the sun. Several of them were nude. If they had any reaction to the newcomer seeing them undressed, they didn't show it.

They continued to the front edge of the deck, where a Hispanic woman sat at a table under an umbrella. Gemma was awestruck by her. She had a massive tattoo, all in black ink, of a lion covering her entire left shoulder and upper arm. A cow skull decorated her forearm, and a bobcat was on the back of her hand. The Virgin Mary stood proudly displayed on her chest above her breasts. Her hair was black but was pulled into two long braids, which were bright green. She wore a white bikini that left three-fourths of her breasts exposed. Her legs were stretched out, feet on the chair next to her. Her bikini bottoms were maybe two inches wide. A tuft of black pubic hair peeked out from the top.

"Tawney, this is Gemma, the girl I told you about last night. Gemma, this is Tawney. I'll leave you two to talk."

Reesie walked over to one of the groups of women on the far side of the deck. Tawney pulled her feet off the chair and gestured to it.

"Please, sit." She pronounced sit *seet*. Her Spanish accent wasn't too thick, and Gemma suspected Tawney deployed it on purpose. "Would you like a drink? A water? Something stronger?"

"No, I'm good for right now."

"Suit yourself. It's going to be hot today. You will get thirsty."

"I'll get something later if that's okay."

"Sure. So, what did Reesie tell you about what we're doing here?"

Gemma glanced over at Reesie, who was rubbing suntan lotion onto the back of one of the nude women. "She said it was porn, but not the typical porn."

"Have you done porn before?"

"No. I've been stripping for a couple of years, and we've done some live sex shows. I've done some out calling too."

"So, you're a stripper and a prostitute."

Gemma opened her mouth to protest but thought about what she did last night to get one more night in a shitty motel and stopped herself. "Yeah, I guess I am."

Tawney waved her hand toward the other women on the deck. "We've all done our share of both. I fucked my way from Buenos Aires to Los Angeles, and I've done plenty of fucking and stripping to stay here. Reesie said you were turned down for a job at the Brass Pole?"

"I've been turned down everywhere."

"It's this economy. Everyone is working a few rungs lower than they used to. It's pushed many of us off the pole because these women who still think they will make it as actresses are desperate and work for nothing. Some clubs are milking them for two-thirds of their take. It's hard to make ends meet at that rate. It's why I started doing some research, and I have some thoughts on how to earn money without having to climb back on the pole.

"What do you know about sex cams?"

Gemma had heard of them. A couple of web services had cropped up, allowing women to do live sex shows over the internet from their houses. "I know the basics. I don't know how they get paid or anything, though." She looked around. "It must pay well if you can afford this place."

Tawney laughed. "This isn't my place. It belongs to a movie guy. A *slash*. As in producer slash director slash writer. He travels nine months of the year for his movies. I—well, *we*—fuck him a few times whenever he's here, and he lets me house sit for him. We don't trash the place, he gets all the sex he wants, and we have a place to do our business. It's a—what do you call it—symbiotic relationship."

"It's a nice place. A lot nicer than the shithole I'm staying in."

"How would you like to stay here?"

Gemma's heart jumped. "To be honest, I'd do just about anything to not go back to that motel. I can't fuck the manager again for the price of a room."

Tawney smiled. "Well, I need to learn more about you, and we'll have to do a screen test. Do you eat pussy?"

The redhead from the frat house flashed through her mind. "Yes."

Tawney stood up and pulled the strings on her bikini, removing the small swatch of fabric and exposing her labia to Gemma. They were clean, with a thick patch of hair sculpted into a triangle above them. She sat back down and spread her legs. "Take off your clothes and come over here."

Gemma heard footsteps and two women approached with cameras held out in front of them. She hesitated.

Tawney was playing with her pussy, pulling the lips apart and sliding a finger through the slit. "We're rolling here, Gemma. This is showtime. Your future is waiting."

Five
Present Day

We had finished getting ready by the time Gemma got to the part where she was about to eat Argentinean pussy. I wore a crop top that cinched under my breasts. It had off-the-shoulder sleeves, and I went bra-less, as I often do. Some people think that makes your tits sag, but it's actually the opposite. Having a bra hold them up all the time weakens the muscles and causes them to sag faster. Or at least that's the latest theory I'd read, and since it agreed with my lifestyle, I chose to believe it. I had on a tight mini skirt and three-inch heels. Hey, we were going to a strip club. Heels were part of the dress code.

Gemma wore a black skirt with a backless animal print top and also chose a pair of three-inch heels. "I'm a little nervous," she said. "It's been a long time since I've been to Poppa Chubby's."

"When was the last time?"

"The night after I met you. I never went back after I left for LA."

"So, Tawney is there? Or Reesie?"

"Ashleigh."

"Oh, that's right. The one who you worked with at Poppa Chubby's, and then in LA."

"Yeah. When Tawney got things going out there, we needed more girls. And it was easy, fun work, so I called Ashleigh and convinced her to come out."

"Ah. And why did she move back here, of all places?"

"Why did you and I both move back here within the last year? It's home. But what pushed *her* to leave LA after a decade out west? We'll have to ask her what the deal is when we get there. She just told me that the whole company is in trouble." Gemma fluffed up her hair. "You ready?"

"Yes. Let's do this."

"Here we are," Gemma said. She gestured toward the big sign that read "Poppa Chubby's Gentleman's Club" in blaring neon. The building stood out not just from the blast of color but also because everything around it was so drab. Rundown buildings on either side looked vacant, with broken windows and weeds taking over the parking lots.

"Nice neighborhood," I observed.

"Yeah, well, it wasn't much better back in the day, either. Tough economy then, tough economy now."

"And yet people always have money for the strip club."

Gemma smiled. "Strip clubs and liquor stores. Depression proof."

She pulled into the lot, parked in a spot near the door, and we got out. We could hear *Megatron* by Nicki Minaj pumping before we even got to the door. Gemma looked at me. "Well, here goes nothing. I haven't darkened the door of this place in ten years. I'm a little nervous."

"We'll be fine. I've got your back."

She laughed and pulled the door open. The music was about twenty decibels louder with the door open. I did not miss having to shout over the music to talk to people in clubs.

"Baby girl!"

Before I knew what was happening, a massive black man grabbed Gemma and pulled her into a fierce hug.

"Andre! I can't believe you're still here!"

"Yeah, you know, they can't afford to let me go. Shit, baby girl, I thought I'd never see you again. I missed you around here."

"I can't believe you remember me! I'm sorry I left without saying goodbye. It was... complicated.

34

Hey, why do they have you working the door? If you're up here, who's watching the girls?"

Andre smiled, flashing an impossible number of teeth. "My boy, Andre."

Gemma's jaw dropped. "Little Andre? He was just a skinny little thing!"

"You been gone a long time, baby girl. He's twenty-one now, an inch taller than me, and twenty pounds of muscle heavier. Goes by AJ for Andre Junior. He takes good care of the girls. I hurt my knee a few years back, bouncing a fool who got too handsy. I had surgery, leg brace, all that noise. But you know how it is; I got mouths to feed, so Poppa put me up here at my same salary. He didn't have to do that, so I'm grateful for this spot. I hope Little Chub keeps me here when he takes over."

Gemma gave him the same look a quizzical dog would give. "Little Chub? Is Poppa retiring?"

Andre nodded. "Yep. Gino is taking over, and he's not like his dad. No loyalty, fancies himself a gangster, I think, because he was born into this line of business. I worry for my future with him at the controls. I find myself on the outside looking in more and more lately."

"I'm sure he'll take care of you," Gemma assured him.

"Maybe. We'll see. Poppa will put in a word for me if nothing else. For what that's worth."

Gemma finally looked over at me. "Andre, this is my girlfriend, Darcy. We're here to see Ashleigh. Er, Mercedes. Is she here?"

It sent a thrill through me to hear her introduce me as her girlfriend with no reservations. For his part, Andre didn't even blink. He just reached his massive hand out to me. "Darcy, it's a pleasure to meet you. You'd better be good to baby girl. She's one of the good ones. I may have a bum leg, but I'll bounce you good if you hurt her."

I shook his hand, which was surprisingly soft. His threat was delivered with a smile. I thought it was cute he was assuming the role of protector for someone he hadn't seen in a decade. "It's nice to meet you, too, Andre. I'll do my best to take care of her."

He turned back to Gemma. "And to answer your question, yes, Ashleigh is here. She's been back for a week now, working on her routine. She's going to reveal it tonight, in just a few minutes, actually."

He stood straighter, and his face became less jovial, sterner. I followed his gaze and saw an equally tall, equally muscled white man walking toward us. He wore an ill-fitting suit that looked like it would split open if he flexed his muscles. If you asked central casting to send over a wannabe mafia enforcer, this is who they would send.

"What's up, Joey?" Andre asked as the man approached.

Of course, his name was Joey. He looked like a Joey.

"Poppa wants to see these girls at his table. Now."

Gemma looked at me and grimaced. "I was hoping to avoid this."

"You'll be alright, baby girl. He missed you, too. He may not have shown it, but he has a heart, and you might have broken it when you left. He'll be glad to see you. It's good you came before he's run out the door by his boy!"

"Come with me, please," Joey commanded and started walking to the left side of the club. Gemma fell in line behind him, and I followed her.

He led us over to a table with a man and woman sitting with their backs to the wall, watching the activity in the club. I took a minute to look around as we approached the table. The bar was against the wall by the entry. It seemed an odd place to put it, but then I realized if someone was going to sit and drink, they weren't tipping the dancers, so they probably didn't want to give up the premium space near the stages.

On the opposite wall was a series of doors which I *think* were marked with VIP on them. It was hard to tell in the dim lighting from this distance.

A dozen tables were lined up across the middle of the room, all occupied with people eating dinner. I never understood the idea of going to a strip club for a meal, but people seemed to do it. Several waitresses wearing black panties with pink lace trim and matching bras buzzed around, taking orders and dropping off drinks and food.

I spotted the bathrooms in the corner opposite us, and straight ahead, against the wall, was the DJ booth.

At the front of the room were three stages. Each one was about six feet wide, and the ones on the outside were just long rectangles with a brass pole at either end. About eight feet up, another brass pole connected the two horizontally. The center stage was longer and ended with a large round platform. I chuckled. It looked like a penis. I was sure that was intentional.

The song ended, and the girls on stage collected their money and skittered away behind a curtain. The DJ made an announcement. *"Gentlemen, and ladies, we're going to take a short break. Get up, go to the bathroom, hit the ATM, and get ready, because returning to Poppa Chubby's is a favorite from back in the day! You regulars—I'm looking at you, Rodney—"*

The man who must have been Rodney screamed, "Yeah! Woo!"

"—will remember her name. Get ready for the triumphant return of Mercedes!"

He said it like "Mer SAY deeeees," and the people gathered around the stage whooped and yelled. Apparently, a lot of them either remembered her, or they just liked yelling. The music returned at a lower volume. This time the DJ selected *Cold Shot* by Stevie Ray Vaughan.

We arrived at the table, and Joey pulled out a chair for Gemma, at the right of the man I assumed to be Poppa Chubby and another next to Gemma for me. We scooted our chairs in and situated ourselves, so we were looking at the couple.

Poppa Chubby was tall in his chair—I guessed him to be six-three, six-four, or taller—and was also fat. If he was less than three hundred pounds, I'd eat my napkin. He had wavy black hair, held up in a pompadour by a considerable amount of hair gel, or maybe it was Pomade. His hair was gray on the sides and descended into two-inch wide sideburns that stopped an inch past the bottom of his ears. He played with an unlit cigar. He wore a black shirt with stitching on the pockets that reminded me of something Johnny Cash would have worn.

He pointed the cigar at Gemma. "I knew my eyes didn't deceive me. I told Olena, 'that looks like my Alexis.' Didn't I tell you that, Olena?"

The woman next to him said, "Yes, Poppa, you told me that." She had a distinctly eastern European accent, had long, black hair, bright blue eyes, and

Angelina Jolie's lips. She wore what was essentially a fancy bikini top. It was white with dual straps that went over her shoulders and disappeared under the cascade of black hair. The bra itself was almost a tube top, but the straps were needed to hold her massive breasts aloft and pulled together. Between the straps, the fabric swooped down, creating a canyon of cleavage. A half-moon cut out at the bottom of the bra showed some of her ample underboob. What really struck me, though, were her tattoos.

From each collarbone to the back of both hands, she was covered with them. Spiderwebs, flowers, pistols, faces—they all ran together. Her right shoulder looked like it had an image from a Russian propaganda poster from the 1940s. On each collarbone rested a swallow. From what I could see— which was a lot—her huge breasts had no ink on them, but underneath them was the word "Welcome" in a sprawling, old English font. I have no idea why, but I found myself quite attracted to this spectacle of a woman. I felt that familiar tingle in my pussy and couldn't help but stare at her.

Poppa continued talking. "This must be reunion week. First Mercedes comes back, and now my Alexis. Such interesting timing."

I was a little creeped out by the way he said that. He was like a corpulent, sideburn-wearing version of Gollum. I held my tongue because Poppa

Chubby didn't strike me as someone who had a great sense of humor.

Gemma turned to me. "Alexis was my stage name."

"You look good, Alexis," Poppa continued. "If anything, you're better looking now than you were ten years ago. Why'd you leave, girl? Why didn't you say goodbye at least?"

"I knew you'd talk me into staying, and I had to go. I met someone, and I was afraid to show them who I was back then. I tried to run from myself."

He laughed. "And when you got wherever you were going, there you were, right?"

"Something like that, yeah."

He studied his cigar for a minute. "Yeah, well, I hope he was worth it. Did you ever get things settled with this guy, the one who took you away from Poppa?"

Gemma looked at me. "Yeah, I did. It took a long time, but we reconnected when we were supposed to."

His eyes flicked back and forth between us. "Oh, it's like that, then." He scanned me from my curly red locks down to my tits, which he was no doubt picturing without my top. "I've always loved redheads. Never had enough of them on the poles." He caught himself and put his hand on Olena's tattooed arm. "But my heart belongs to this raven-haired beauty. Alexis, and—I'm sorry, what's your name?"

"Darcy," I said.

"Darcy. Meet my wife, Olena Tartaryn. She's from Ukraine. We just got married!"

Olena stood. Her dress was a bikini bottom, cut low enough that I knew she waxed everything, with opaque white linen attached to the lower hem of the bikini brief. Her entire muscular, defined abdomen was tattooed. She had roses under the WELCOME, some things I couldn't discern filling the dead space, and skulls on each hip, their grimaces peeking out from under the bikini fabric. I don't know what it was—maybe it was because I'd never seen a woman so inked up, but I found myself wondering if she was tattooed all the way down to her vagina. I felt my face flush. This Ukrainian woman had a spell on me. "Hello, I am Olena," she said. She leaned over the table and extended her hand.

Gemma reached out and shook her hand. "Hi, I'm Gemma. Congratulations on your wedding."

"Thank you."

I stood and reached for her hand. "Hi, Darcy. I'm Olena. Er, I mean, I'm Darcy. You're Olena. Um, congratulations on your wedding, too." *Real smooth, Darce.*

"Thank you, Darcy. I love your gorgeous red hair. You're a vision, I could eat you alive. Gemma is

42

lucky girl." Olena turned to Poppa. "I go to the office now."

She walked toward a door near the DJ booth, her hips swaying seductively as she did so. I think I might have actually drooled.

Gemma was giving me a look that said, *what the fuck?* I returned a slight shrug. *Fuck if I know what that was about.*

Poppa turned his attention back to Gemma. "You heard about the changes here at the club?"

Gemma nodded. "Yeah, Andre said you're retiring. That took me by surprise. I didn't think you were the retiring type."

"Yeah, well, I'm a fucking senior citizen now. Sixty-five years old. I know I ain't got a long time left on this planet. What do I have? Maybe ten more years where I can get it up? Once there's no lead in the pencil, what's the fucking point, you know? I want to spend that time with Olena, not in this place." He contemplated the cigar. "Jesus, I can't even smoke in here anymore, thanks to the city regulations. In my own fucking club!"

"Whose club?"

A man walked behind Gemma and Poppa Chubby and took the seat that Olena had just vacated. He looked like he was about forty years old and had the build of a weightlifter, with broad shoulders and thick arms that filled the sleeves of his sport coat. He wore a t-shirt under the coat that read *Parental Advisory: Explicit Content.* He completed his outfit with jeans and black Chuck Taylor All-stars.

"Did I just hear you call this *your* club, Pop?"

"Girls, this is my boy, the new owner of Poppa Chubby's. He used to go by Little Chub, but now he wants to be known as Gino. His real name is Walter."

Gino made a face. "Thanks, Pop. Or should I say *Norman*. Dopey names run in this family, I guess, don't they?"

"Settle down, *Gino*. Do you remember Alexis?"

He squinted at Gemma, accessing his memory banks. "Oh, yeah! You've kept yourself up well! You need a job?"

"No, thank you, though, Gino. We're here to see Ashleigh. Or, Mercedes."

"Oh, she hasn't gone on yet? Awesome. I wanted to see this."

His timing was perfect because the familiar grinding guitar opening to *Kickstart My Heart* by Motley Crue faded in while Stevie Ray faded out. The volume continued to increase, and the DJ looped the intro to extend it. The lights dimmed, and overhead spotlights focused their beams on the center stage. I saw Joey walk over and take a position at the base of the stage.

"Alright, Poppa's Chubbies, get your money ready because Mercedes is about to hit the center

stage. Back from her world tour of pleasure, she's ready to kick! Start! Your! Heart!"

When Vince Neil started singing, Ashleigh exploded through the curtain. Both arms were sleeved with tattoos; those on the left arm were all in color, and on the right were grayscale. She wore a silver sequined bikini that barely contained her huge breasts and silver platform shoes with six-inch heels. She did a series of back handsprings like a gymnast on a tumbling run. How she did that with those shoes, I will never know. As she approached the big circular end of the stage, she leaped into the air and landed about halfway up on the pole, sideways, crossing her arms and grabbing onto it, body crouched in a squatting position, her heels hooked over the brass, and she swung around it a couple of times. She was defying gravity.

Gemma leaned into me and said, "That move's called the Spider."

That made sense. Ashleigh did look like a spider perched sideways on the pole.

Gemma continued. "No one mounts the pole like that. If you miss, you end up off the end of the stage with a broken leg, and you're lucky if you don't put someone's eye out with a heel. I would never attempt it. She's fearless."

"She's fucking amazing!" I shouted back. Despite my latent jealousy of Ashleigh's prior relationship with Gemma, she had me riveted twenty seconds into her routine.

"Just watch. If I know her, it'll only get better."

Ashleigh spun faster, threw her legs out straight, held her body horizontally, and did the splits.

Gemma kept up her commentary like a sportscaster. "The Iron X."

Ashleigh pulled one leg through her arms, then did the splits pressed against the pole. She inverted herself, slid down the brass, stopped and held herself up with one arm, and rotated, so she was parallel with the stage. She opened her legs and dropped to the deck, doing the splits again, bouncing her pussy on the stage.

Gemma continued her narration as if I was going to remember any of the technical terms. Until this moment, I didn't even know pole dancing *had* technical terms! "A Marion Amber into a Pole Split, followed by a Keen, One-armed Hand-stand, and a Bounce Split."

The amount of core strength and flexibility these moves had to take was beyond anything I could contemplate. This was incredible. The men in the audience were screaming and shouting, literally throwing money onto the stage.

Ashleigh scaled the pole again. At the top, I saw her loosen the knot on her sequined top. She grabbed the horizontal pole and swung away from the vertical one. She released one hand, rotated one hundred eighty degrees, caught the pole, and released the other hand. She did this, over and over, moving from the pole at the front of the stage toward the one at the back. Her legs spread wide into the splits, and she started rotating faster and faster, her legs becoming a blur.

"The Helicopter," Gemma said.

Ashleigh's bikini top flew off about halfway to the rear pole, landing on a guy's head. He grabbed it and stood up, whipping it around over his head and shouting. His friends grabbed him and pulled him back into his seat.

Once she reached the rear pole, she grabbed it with one hand and slowly slid down, rotating around the pole as she did so.

"One-armed spin-out," Gemma told me.

Ashleigh lifted her legs, pointing them straight out, and opened them wide. She put her other hand into her bikini and began playing with her pussy. The men went berserk. Money showered the stage. As she approached the bottom, she pulled her hand out of the bikini and put her arm behind her, anchoring her elbow on the deck, her hand holding her hips off the platform, her head and shoulders resting on the ground, the pole in the crook of her neck. She did the splits with her legs held in the air and shoved her free hand into her bikini bottoms again. As the song slowed down for the drop, Ashleigh masturbated through the entire middle thirty seconds of the song. Her hips bucked in time to the music, giving the illusion that she was fucking her hand, and the center of her bikini grew dark with her juices. The men on that side of the stage were going absolutely wild, shoving to get to the front. One of them tried to leap onto the stage, and Joey grabbed him by the belt and yanked him back. Now I knew why he moved over there as the music started up. The crowd was nearly rioting.

"I don't know what that was," Gemma said.

"The Levitating Pussy Playhouse," I shouted. I looked over my shoulder and saw Gemma laughing.

When the song's tempo picked back up, Ashleigh rotated into another bounce split, and I saw her tug at the strings on her bikini bottoms. She did a smooth rise from the splits to a standing position, scaled the pole, did a few more maneuvers, and slid down into the splits again. She bounced up and did another set of backward handsprings, in the middle of which her bikini flew off, and a couple of guys fought to grab it. The winner held it aloft like a trophy, then pressed it to his face and reveled in everything his prize had to offer.

Ashleigh again mounted the pole in a leap, but this time swung her body around and around, opening her legs and letting the room see her bare vagina. As the song ended, she dropped to the stage, the song's final note coinciding with her pussy hitting the platform. All the lights turned off at that exact instant and came back on five or six seconds later.

Ashleigh was gone. The place erupted in a chorus of cheers, and even though there was no one on stage, people still tossed money. Two club workers ran over with push brooms and quickly shuffled the small mountain of cash to the rear of the stage and under the curtain. There must have been over a thousand dollars in that pile, collected in just over four minutes.

Gino was impressed. "Now *that* was a fucking show! Holy shit-balls, that bitch can dance!" Without saying goodbye, he got up and walked to the office door where Olena had disappeared a few minutes before.

"You'd think he hadn't spent half his life in a strip club," Poppa lamented, shaking his head.

A huge black man bearing a strong resemblance to Andre approached us. "Gemma?" he said, looking me in the eye. I shook my head and pointed over my shoulder. He redirected his eyes to her. "Gemma? Mercedes, I mean, Ashleigh said you can come back now."

Gemma stood and gave Poppa a hug. "It's good to see you, Poppa. Congrats again on your wedding!"

49

He smiled. "Be good, darling. I'm proud of you. I'm glad you got out of this life."

She gave his shoulder a squeeze and turned to the black man. "Lead on, Andre."

"My dad is Andre. I go by AJ."

"Sorry, AJ."

He smiled. "No worries. Come on, follow me."

Six

AJ led us past the bathrooms and through a curtain. A set of four steps to our left led up to a walkway. This was where the strippers went to get to the three stages. Thick cushions covered the walls behind the curtain and the door through which we were about to walk. I wondered what they were for, but when the door shut behind us, the noise from the club was cut by two-thirds. Soundproofing. I was learning a lot tonight.

"Summer, Saphire, Phoenix, you're up!"

A trio of women in bikinis scurried toward the door at AJ's command. If they were in order, Summer was a tall blonde with chiseled abs and a single star tattoo above her left hip. Saphire was a shorter black woman with huge breasts and tribal tattoos that ran down each hip and touched right above her vagina, and her right arm was sleeved. Phoenix was a light-skinned version of Gemma with raven-black hair and was unique among these women in that she had no tattoos.

As the three women left, Ashleigh came walking out of a room to the right of the entry. It had no door, only a curtain, and I could see sinks, toilet stalls, and showers beyond them. Ashleigh was nude, using a towel to wipe off her arms. She squealed and ran to Gemma, wrapping her in a wet, naked embrace. My jealousy flared up again.

"Oh, Gemma, it's so good to see you! My god, you look great!" She turned her gaze to me. "Who's this?"

"This is Darcy, my girlfriend."

In an unexpected move, Ashleigh closed the distance between us and pulled me tight to her. She was strong and pressed her naked honeydew-sized breasts into my... grapefruits. She smelled like cinnamon and vanilla. It reminded me of how Gemma smelled the night we met in that frat house basement so long ago. God, that smell is delicious.

"Ooh, no bra. You're teasing me," Ashleigh said. "You must be something special if you've got Gemma introducing you as her girlfriend. It's a passive-aggressive way of letting everyone know you're both off the market."

She released the embrace and brushed her hands over my nipples as she pulled her arms back. Against my will, they poked against the fabric of my crop top.

"Tell me about L.A.," Gemma said, "and Tawney. You said she was getting in trouble."

I could tell that Gemma was either mad or nervous because she was really direct and to the point.

Ashleigh looked sideways at AJ, standing guard by the door. "We're good in here, AJ. I need some alone time with these sexy ladies."

AJ shook his head, smiled, and walked out, leaving us alone in the locker room.

"I like him, but he lingers a little too much, you know? He doesn't have the same boundaries as his dad did. Feels like he's always listening in. Plus, I'm pretty sure he's fucking some of them, and Andre would never do that. Anyway, come on," Ashleigh said. With her bare ass swaying seductively, she led us to a make-up station with a locker standing next to it. She spun the dial on a combo lock and opened the locker, then reached in and pulled out the world's smallest tartan G-string and matching skirt. "You'll have to forgive me while I get ready for my tour on the floor."

She sat on the stool and rubbed her labia furiously, looking back and forth between Gemma and me. "Fuck, this is kind of hot. I wish we had time for a quick threesome. Darcy, I bet you taste like honey. And I *love* your hair!"

I looked uncomfortably at Gemma, and she gave me a tiny shrug. Ashleigh slid her legs into the G-String and pulled it tight, giving herself a camel-toe. Her swollen labia hung out of either side of the tiny garment. She fastened the skirt around her waist, all of four inches of fabric covering nothing of interest. She looked in the mirror and smiled. "I'll be in the VIP room in about a minute in this outfit. You know, Gemma, as much as I liked working with Tawney, I missed this. Maybe I'll feel different in a month, but I love the screaming and shouting and the live feedback of *real people*, you know? Versus the *'cha-ching'* of online tips. I don't know. Maybe it was just time for a change of scenery."

Gemma was growing impatient. "Ash, what's going on?"

Ashleigh stood and grabbed her phone from the countertop. The charging cable had little lights in it that moved, making it look like energy flowed from the black square charger emblazoned with "Obi-Tech" to the phone itself. She unplugged it, and the lights turned off. "Here. Read this."

She opened an email and handed the phone to Gemma. I peeked over her shoulder while Ashleigh busied herself applying makeup.

> *Hi Ash... I don't know what to tell you other than we've all been screwed here. I've given you all the money I can. I still have girls here that need paid, and our cash reserves are almost gone. As in stolen! I can't give you what I don't have. I'm going to be lucky to pay the mortgage on this*

place. If we can't get this fixed, we're going to be out on the street.

Please know, Ash, I'm going to do everything I can to make this right to you. To everyone. I just have to sort out what's happening and who's behind it, then hopefully we can get everything back, or at least some of it.

And please don't involve Gemma. She's out of this life. There's no need to drag her back into this stuff. Besides, she's a finance guru, not a cop. We need someone who can investigate fraud and identity theft. If we had a tax problem, I'd call her.

I don't want to do more via email. If you need to talk, please call me.

XOXO
Tawney

Gemma's brow furrowed. "So, what's going on? Who's stealing you guys' money?"

Ashleigh shrugged. "No one knows. It was small at; first, a few hundred was pulled from the company account. Tawney thought it was a mistake and called the bank. They said it was an international transfer and that she had done it. Tawney swears she didn't. So, she filed a fraud complaint and changed the password on the account. The next week several thousand went missing. She called the police, but they said someone using the password had processed it. And you can guess that the cops weren't under a lot of pressure from the mayor to help a bunch of sex workers.

"So, I needed to get paid, and the clubs in LA weren't hiring. Plus, Tawney had been making comments that I was aging out. Can you believe that shit? I'm fucking thirty-six! Prime MILF age. There's a huge market for that stuff. You saw my routine tonight! How many girls you know could stick that opening mount?" She flexed her stomach, the six-pack showing through. "Do these look like the abs of someone aging out?" She grabbed my hands and put them on her tits. "Are these aging out?"

I had minimal experience with breast implants. Ashleigh's tits were huge, and while they hung with a natural teardrop shape, there wasn't much sag for breasts this large, so I assumed they were fake.

"Well?" Ashleigh demanded. "They feel good, right?"

"Uh, yeah."

"And they weren't cheap, either. Half the people that get their hands on them can't tell whether or not they're real. Tawney's about ten minutes younger than me. Aging out my ass."

Gemma pulled my hands away from Ashleigh's massive mammaries. "That's enough, Al Franken. She'll have you fingering her next to see how tight her pussy is."

Ashleigh laughed while she put on a tartan bikini top. "She'll need to use her tongue to get a true measure. You both should, and then you can compare notes."

I was thinking about the fact that this woman eagerly wanted to fuck both Gemma and me. I wondered how much of an issue it was going to be with her living in town again. Gemma directed the conversation back to business.

"Focus, Ashleigh. You needed to get paid so...."

"Oh, yeah, so I called Gino. I figured after ten years in LA, I could come back here and clean up. He told me to come back and see how it goes for a week. And I just fucking nailed my first show. I bet I grossed twelve hundred out there. Net seven hundred or so after the club takes its cut. Plus, I have floor duty, VIP rooms... I'm gonna be alright. I still have about half my camming audience, too."

"So, if Tawney doesn't want me involved, and you're all set up here, why'd you bring this to me?'

"You helped her set up the whole organization, and you have the head for numbers. She doesn't. As pissed as I am about her insulting my age and maybe stealing my money, she was good to work with until recently. I think she's just incredibly stressed. She's losing girls right and left, and that's just making her cash flow problem worse. She needs you, Gem. All the girls out there need help. Someone's taking advantage of them, and that's not right."

Gemma looked at me. "Fancy a trip to LA?"

I smiled. "My detective skills are rusty, but I go where you go."

Ashleigh put her phone back on the charging cable, and the little lights started moving again. The door opened, and AJ poked his head in.

"Everything alright in here?"

Ashleigh leaned around us. "Yeah, AJ! I'm coming."

"Okay. Just checking."

Ashleigh smiled. "It was good to see you, Gem. I hope you can help them figure it out!" She turned her eyes to me, leering like a she-wolf. "And it was good to meet you, Darcy. I wish we had more time to get to know each other! But, I have to go strut my stuff."

We walked with her back to the club floor. When we got to the curtain, she quickly turned and kissed Gemma full on the mouth and slid a hand under my shirt, squeezing my right breast and rolling the nipple between her fingers. I was too shocked to react, and apparently, Gemma was too.

Ashleigh broke off the kiss and released my boob. "I missed you, Gem." She looked at me and smiled like the devil. "Now we're titty sisters. One day we'll be pussy pals."

She turned and walked through the curtain. Gemma and I just looked at each other for a moment. For once, we were both speechless.

Yeah, Ashleigh was going to make things more complicated.

Seven

There was no mistaking Tawney when we arrived at the baggage claim. The five-foot-eight Hispanic woman wore white fishnet leggings under white leather hot pants, a white leather bikini top, and large gold hoop earrings. Her black hair turned a vivid pink after the first six inches and was styled into two long pink Dutch braids that hung down to the small of her back. The three-inch heels brought her height close to six feet. And if that wasn't enough, there were dozens of tattoos all over her body, including a twelve-inch lion's head, complete with flowing mane, that covered her entire upper left arm.

"I've never seen so much ink in my life as I've seen in the past thirty-six hours."

Gemma smiled. "I made myself stand out by *not* getting any ink. Some of the girls just overdo it, but some, like Tawney," she threw me a sideways glance, "or Olena look sexy as fuck all inked up."

"I won't argue there. It's hypnotic or something."

Gemma caught Tawney's eye, and the woman flashed a bright white set of teeth, looking very much like a predator which had just caught sight of its prey. She took long steps toward us, like a runway model, crossing her feet as she walked, making her hips sway up and down. I noticed almost everyone in the vicinity was watching her. She commanded attention.

She and Gemma practically collided in an embrace, and Tawney gave her a long, tongue-filled kiss. She had a sultry Spanish accent. "Gemma, baby, it's been too long! I never should have let you go!"

My jealousy program was activated, but Tawney shut it down by grabbing me and planting the same kiss on me. Her mouth was electric and sent a current to the bottom of my feet and back. Her tongue tasted like a candy cane. She broke off the kiss but kept her face inches from mine. "And you, *pelirroja,* redheads are my weakness. Gemma had better keep an eye on you, or I'll steal you away from her and make you mine. You'll never want another woman after I'm finished with you."

"Uh... thanks?" I didn't know what else to say. I'd be lying if I said my pussy wasn't wet after that.

Gemma and Tawney both started laughing. "Let go of her, Tawney. You're freaking her out."

Tawney laced her fingers through mine, and we followed Gemma to the carousel to wait for our bags. "I'm sorry, Darcy. Gemma told me so much about you, I had to make a grand entrance. I mean, you're the woman who sent her to California with her tail between her legs! If it wasn't for you, I never would have met her. And you two still wound up together. It's a fucking beautiful story, girl. A fairy tale. I wasn't kidding, though; I do love redheads, and you are straight gorgeous. Gemma's a lucky girl." She glanced around. "Look at how many boners there are here. God, I should hand out business cards."

I laughed as I saw several guys adjusting their stances to hide the tents they were pitching in their pants after the show we just put on. I had a feeling Tawney got that reaction when she went about anywhere.

With our bags rolling along at our sides, we headed for the parking lot. I was trying to guess what kind of car Tawney would drive. I suspected some sort of flashy convertible, likely red or yellow, so I was surprised when she led us to a silver BMW 550 Gran Turismo. She popped the hatch so we could stash our suitcases, then climbed in.

"Do you guys want to get something to eat—" Tawney started.

"In-N-Out," Gemma said. She looked back at me. "Does that sound good?"

I smiled. It had been forever since I'd been there. "That would be awesome."

Tawney nodded. "Okay, I can deal with that. There's one on Sunset not far from the house. It'll be an hour or more before we get there. You okay with that?"

"Sure," Gemma answered. "You can fill us in on what's going on while we drive and sit in traffic."

Tawney set the address in Waze, backed out of the parking space, and was on the gas. I don't want to say that she drove recklessly, but she tested the G-force capabilities of the precision German engineering built into her car several times.

"Let's see, where should I start?" Tawney mused. "I guess first I'll tell you the situation. We're in a different house than we were in when you were last working with us, Gemma. The producer who owned our other place got married, and his wife wasn't too cool with a sex cam studio operating out of her house. But, he knew a director who was in the midst of a *me too* situation, and he needed to free up some cash. He bought this place in 2009 for a huge discount—like nine million bucks, and today it's worth fifteen million—and he didn't want to lose it if he got sued. So he transferred the deed to a trust and leased it to us, in effect having us take over his mortgage payments."

"Which are how much?" Gemma asked.

"Thirty thousand a month."

"Holy shit! Thirty *thousand dollars?* That's insane! You'd have my house paid off in three months!"

Gemma looked over her shoulder and smiled at me. "It's California, Darce. Hollywood Hills. You get someone that makes twenty million a movie, thirty grand a month is pocket change." She returned her focus to Tawney. "Ashleigh talked like you owned the place, said you were at risk of losing it."

Tawney shook her head. "No, that's not exactly right. The director still owns it, or his trust does. We're leasing it, but there's a clause if we miss two payments, the trust can look for a new tenant and kick us out. And we've missed one already."

"So tell me about that. What's happened to your cash?"

I couldn't contain myself. "Thirty *thousand* dollars? Why wouldn't you find another place way cheaper?"

"We'll give you a tutorial on the industry later, Darce. Tawney, please, what happened?"

"Well, one day, I saw a transfer to an overseas account of five hundred bucks. I assumed it was a mistake, so I called the bank. When I told them it wasn't me, they jumped into action and got their fraud team involved, but they said the transfer was processed using the account password, so there was nothing they could do. They told me to use a sixteen-digit password to better secure my account.

"So I did that. I set this impossible-to-remember password and thought things were okay. Then a week later, ten thousand dollars was gone. This time I called the cops. They dug into it, but again, it was done using the password, and the routing was to a bank in Buenos Aires."

Gemma's face registered shock. "Oh, shit, I see where this is going."

"Yup. They started investigating *me.*"

I was confused and must have looked like it because Gemma looked at me in the back seat and took a minute to explain it to me. "Tawney is originally from Buenos Aires. I assume once they found that out, they shifted from trying to figure out who did it to trying to prove it was Tawney."

Tawney glanced at me in the rear-view mirror. "Yep, that's exactly what happened. The only thing that saved me was their IT guys put something—a sniffer, or snooper, or something like that—on my internet connection. When the next hit happened, and we lost fifty thousand, they confirmed I hadn't accessed any bank in Buenos Aires."

Gemma assumed the answer to the next question. "But they didn't find the thieves."

"No. And this was having a huge effect on us. I pulled out fifty grand to pay the girls with, but the money kept disappearing. I closed the account and opened a new one, and it started happening there, too.

"Even worse, one of the top-earning girls had her accounts hacked and thousands of dollars taken. So she left, not long after Ashleigh did. When the last payments came in from the cam sites, the money was taken before I even knew it hit the accounts. So, the girls who still had their payments routing to the LLC aren't getting paid. The whole XX Cam organization is about to collapse."

"This may be a stupid question, but why is it called XX Cam? Shouldn't it be XXX?"

Tawney shook her head. "It's XX as opposed to XY. As in female. All the cam shows have women, and if there's a guy, which isn't too often, there's at least two women with him. We wanted it to be woman-centric."

"Ah, that makes sense. So, Gemma, that's why your audition was with Tawney?"

Tawney smiled and answered for her. "Yes. I personally screen all the girls. They have to perform up to my standards. That's one of our additional revenue streams. We film the auditions and put clips on the big porn sites, then sell access to the full videos on our main website. We also do private chats via that site, and we can charge way more than we get from private shows on the cam sites."

I was getting so intrigued by this. "So, how much do the girls make from doing this?"

"Okay, it's set up like this: the girls' accounts direct all their money to the XX Cam LLC account. The top earners pull in anywhere from a thousand to six, seven thousand a day—"

"A *day?*" I was flabbergasted.

"Yeah. Luna has the record – ten thousand, four hundred sixty-five dollars in one day."

"Oh my *god!* Gemma, why did you get out of this business? Jesus!"

Gemma laughed. "Don't fall for the glam. It's not just sitting in front of a camera and rubbing out an orgasm."

"Yeah. You spend maybe three to five hours a day on a live show. Luna was on cam for almost ten to get that record. The rest of your day is spent moderating the chats for other girls, packing and shipping things people buy—"

"Like what do they buy?"

Tawney shrugged her shoulders. "Anything you want to sell. Panties are a real big item. Signed pictures. I sold an outfit to a fitness model in Columbia, Missouri, for a thousand bucks because she thought it was super cute. She wears it in some of her competitions and sends me pictures of her competing in it. It cost me one-fifty."

"I had no idea there was this huge underground economy out there. This is blowing me away."

Gemma turned and faced me. "This is just scratching the surface. Affiliate links bring in a ton of money, uploading videos to the porn sites, the XX Cam tube site makes a couple thousand a month—"

"It's about forty-five hundred now," Tawney corrected.

"Point is," Gemma continued, "there are multiple revenue streams, but the girls have to maintain them. Plus, they have to work out, buy new outfits, come up with new ideas for their shows. And couples make more money than individual girls do, so a lot of the time, they have to work out their show in advance."

"How much did you make when you were doing this?"

"It was a while ago," Gemma hedged.

"She was our number one girl for a while. I probably don't need to tell you this, but Gemma could bring a dead woman to life. Halfway through her interview, I screamed out, 'you're hired, don't stop eating that pussy!'"

Again, I felt a stir of jealousy, but I realized I had no reason to be. "Yeah, I know. She converted me to women. Outside of that crazy, fateful night in the frat house basement, I could count the number of men I've been in with on one hand. I don't have enough digits for the women I've been with."

Tawney looked at me again in the mirror, a smile lighting up her face. "So, you know what I'm talking about! She got people tipping like mad in her shows. The money wasn't as big back then, but she had the goods."

Candid Camera

We pulled into the parking lot for In-n-Out Burger. Our entrance into the restaurant didn't turn as many heads as the scene in LAX. Looking around, Tawney wasn't the only woman with multi-colored hair, nor did she have the most tattoos. Hollywood had desensitized people to the plumage on display.

Eight

The wrappers from our double protein style burgers—burgers wrapped in lettuce rather than a bun—lay crumpled on our trays. There are certainly better burgers to be had, but there's something about In-n-Out that can't be matched. I learned a long time ago if you have a chance to get INO, don't pass it up.

"It has to be an inside job, right?" Gemma asked Tawney. "How else are they getting the passwords?"

"I've thought of that. But I can't imagine who it could be. When I went into the bank, and they closed the first account and opened a new one for me, they had me set the password at the bank. I didn't write it down; I put it in the password vault on my phone. No one else has access to my phone, so no one could get it that way."

"Still, for them to be using your password, especially the sixteen-digit one, they would have to either be in the house or work at the bank."

"Your PC could have a keylogger virus," Gemma offered.

Tawney shook her head, her pink braids swaying back and forth. "No, we have IT people. I had it checked for viruses. The cops did too."

Gemma's brow was furrowed. "How well do you know all the girls?"

Tawney frowned. "Most of them I know really well. Some as well as I know you."

"And the others?"

"Less well, but they've worked hard. They've given me no reason not to trust them. We do have a couple of newer girls, Leslie and Kaitlyn, and I know less about them than the others."

Gemma kept probing. "Have any of them—even the ones you know well—had any changes recently? New love interests, deaths in the family, sudden new debts, changes in health, sick parents? Anything that could be a financial stressor?"

"I see what you're getting at. And I don't know. No one's mentioned anything like that. No one has gotten a new car. I've not seen any changes in anyone's behavior."

I chimed in. "Would they tell you?"

Both women looked at me, surprised because I'd been silent the whole time.

"Why wouldn't they tell me?" Tawney asked.

"Well, you're the boss. If they're having problems and come to you, you might turn them out or cut back on their screen time. Or if they were planning to rob you, they'd know they'd immediately be the prime suspect. So, of course they'd keep it from you. You need a mole to talk to them and feel them out. Is there someone you trust to do some digging?"

"Well, yes, but if someone was stealing from me, they've been stealing from the rest of the girls too. We'd need someone from the outside, someone they haven't stolen from, to gain their trust and let them in on the scam. And if we go that route, I won't be able to trust them."

"You can trust us," Gemma said.

Was she volunteering us to be cam girls?

Tawney shook her head. "I already told them I had a financial expert coming to look into the situation."

Gemma kept pushing. "Did you tell them she was bringing her girlfriend?"

A wide, white-toothed grin spread across Tawney's face. "No, no, I did not."

They were both looking at me like they were starving, and I was a double, protein style. "You're kidding, right? I can't be a cam girl."

Gemma's face turned devious. "Well, the inside woman *was* your idea."

Okay, next time there's a strategy session, keep your mouth shut. For once, I agreed with my brain. But it was too late this time.

Tawney pleaded with me. "You would be doing me a tremendous favor. Please agree to do it. You're right, it might get us a good lead, and we need something to break loose here. The cops and the bank aren't interested in helping us."

"But, I have no idea how to do what you do. I'd be looking at the camera all the time. I—"

Gemma winked at me. "You've been on camera before, remember? You just didn't know it."

I gave her a look that said, *"That's not the same, and you know it."* But I knew it was too late to argue. The decision was made.

Tawney saw my shoulders sag, and she laughed and clapped her hands. "Alright! We have a plan!" She turned to Gemma. "Now, she's going to have to have sex with some of the girls. Are you going to be okay with that?"

Gemma sat up a little straighter. I could tell that she hadn't thought about that bit before. She turned her brown eyes on me. "Are you willing to do that to help Tawney? If you're willing to go that far, I can deal with it. It's just sex. We just have to guard your identity and make sure no one knows you're not a real cam girl."

"If I'm having sex on camera, doesn't that make me a *real* cam girl?"

She laughed. "Touché!"

Tawney reached over and touched my arm. "Does that mean you'll do it?"

I hedged. I wanted to help, Gemma wanted me to help... but it felt like Gemma and I were suddenly like detectives, partners working a case, and no longer lovers. I looked back and forth between them, and they both met my eyes with bright, hopeful eyes and expectant faces.

I sighed. "You're sure you're okay with me sleeping with other women?"

Gemma nodded. "I mean, I'm not going to watch the shows and Jill off to them, but I know where your bed is going to be when this is all over."

I sighed again. "Okay, I'll do it."

Nine

Gemma kissed me full on the mouth, long and deep, for an eternity. When she finally broke our lips apart, she whispered, "I love you for this. When it's over, assuming we get her money back, I'll make Tawney pay for a vacation for the two of us."

"You make it sound like I'm going off to war."

"I've lived this life, remember? I know how intoxicating it can be. But we're dealing with someone who has stolen more than four hundred thousand dollars in total. They're going to be desperate not to get caught. So, you can't let them think for a second you're working for Tawney."

"I understand."

"I'm just saying—you're going to have to do whatever it takes. Don't worry about me or what I'll think. You need to be Darcy the Cam Girl, so whatever you need to do, go for it. No matter what happens, I'll be waiting for you."

I looked at her for a few moments. I was tempted to make a joke, as I usually did during tense moments, but I didn't. I'd never seen her so serious. "I'll do what I can to get information from the girls, and I'll get out. Okay?"

She looked over at Tawney, who was giving us some space. "We'll keep an eye on you, and if anything gets too crazy, I'll pull you out. Okay?"

"Okay. But I'll be fine, Gemma. I did make it almost all the way to thirty without your help. I can make it another week. Or two, whatever it takes. God, don't let it take two weeks."

She kissed me again, pulling on my lower lip, which she knows is my weakness. I kissed her back and felt her tits for good measure. Tawney saw me and laughed. "Come on, lover girl, before you two start fucking in the In-N-Out parking lot."

I grabbed my bag from the back of the BMW and called for an Uber as Tawney sped off like a rally driver. The plan was for them to get to the house where Tawney would introduce Gemma as the financial investigator. She'd tell the girls I was coming to be added to their crew, and I would show up a few minutes later in my Uber. The fun would begin from there.

The Uber arrived ten minutes later. According to the application on my phone, the driver was a heavyset white woman named Carrie piloting a Honda CRV. I stowed the suitcase in the rear and climbed into the back seat. The trip up the canyon was twisting and turning, and I don't know if it was Carrie's perfume or some sort of air freshener, but something smelled terrible. Between that and the hard corners Carrie was taking, I was feeling carsick for the first time in recent memory.

"I don't get up this way very often," Carrie said. "Most of my calls are downtown, but I was just dropping off another fare at The Magic Castle on Franklin, so I decided to take one call before heading back to LA."

"I guess I was lucky," I said. I cracked the window to get some fresh air, but it only sucked the odor past my face on its way out of the car. Mercifully, after going hard to the left and back to the right three times each, the road straightened out to a series of gentle curves, and I regained control of my stomach.

"Oh, no, someone else would have come along. Oh, shoot, I missed the turn."

She swerved to the edge of the narrow road and made a U-turn, using part of someone's driveway to complete the maneuver. After backtracking a quarter mile, she turned right on Thrasher Avenue, then climbed the narrow road. Tall bushes and trees lined the road, masking the view of many of the huge houses. One place we passed had a shallow driveway that led to three single-car garage doors. Two Mercedes G550's occupied the space. I was not an expert on cars, but I knew that was close to three hundred thousand dollars worth of automobiles sitting there—worth enough to buy my house back home, which had for some reason become my yardstick to measure all forms of wealth. We were definitely in a pricey area.

We continued to wind our way up the hill, slowing for a crew doing road maintenance, pulling to the edge to let someone in a Porsche descend the hill. We reached the apex and began to coast downhill, under a canopy of tree limbs overhanging the road, another hedgerow on the left hiding a house.

The street ended at a T-intersection. The house at the center of the T was Tawney's place—I saw her BMW in the short driveway. In fact, the driveway was all that was visible. A cluster of hedges, palms, and a few other trees I didn't recognize hid everything but the two single-car garage doors. A Lexus occupied the spot next to Tawney's car, a red Range Rover occupied a spot on the street to the right of the driveway, another Mercedes, and a make of car I didn't recognize took spots on the left.

Carrie turned to the right, then made a U-turn to park in front of the driveway. "Here we go! Your friends sure have a nice place here. I bet the view from the back is incredible."

"I hope so," I said. Once I was outside the car and could breathe fresh air, I immediately felt better. Carrie popped the hatch, and I grabbed my bag from the rear. "Thanks so much," I said as I waved at her.

She pulled ahead, then made the left to go back the way we came.

The sidewalk next to the driveway led to a path that ran along the east side of the house. I found the door about twenty-five feet back from the front of the garage and rang the bell. A tall woman opened the door. She had brownish-blonde hair that cascaded in curls down the bottom of her ample breasts. She was topless and wore only a G-String and platform heels below the waist. With those heels, she was an intimidating six-foot-three inches tall. She was gorgeous, with dark brown eyes, full lips, and bright white teeth.

But once again, the most amazing thing about this woman was her tattoos. I thought Olena Tartaryn was covered in ink, but she was a blank canvas compared to this woman. From her feet to her upper thigh, she was covered with images of Hollywood legends. Monroe, Page, Welch, Mansfield. All the great pin-ups and bombshells were represented on her right leg. Her left leg was covered in horror movie icons – Freddie Krueger, Jason, the scary clown guy from that Rob Zombie movie, Hannibal Lecter in that mask.

Her inner, upper thigh, and vagina stood out because of the *lack* of tattoos, though she did have one just visible above the top of the G-string: *Enter At Your Own Risk.*

Her arms were covered in tats of flowers and vines. Similar foliage covered her chest, starting at the top of her breasts and crawling all the way up her neck to her jawline. Her breasts, like her pussy, seemed untouched by ink, but under her fits in a cursive font was a tattoo that read *Hollywood & Vine.*

She was both grotesque and gorgeous. And, like with Olena and Tawney, I felt a twinge down below. *Holy shit, do I have a thing for bad girls? This is new!*

"Hi, I'm Darcy. That's me." *Oh. My. God. Can I ever not be awkward?*

"Hi Darcy, I'm Luna." Her voice was like a soft, warm blanket wrapped in a Spanish accent. "Tawney told me you'd be coming. Come on in!"

I lifted my suitcase and crossed over the threshold, leaving behind Darcy the technical writer, and stepped into the role of Darcy, the newbie cam girl.

Ten

Luna walked in front of me, her back and voluptuous ass cheeks surprisingly free of tattoos. Speaking of her ass, each beautifully round half bobbed up and down independently as she walked. It was hypnotic. She led me to an office where Tawney and Gemma sat by a computer. "Darcy is here. Who's filming?"

The three of us were stunned for a moment. Filming? Filming what?

"Tawney, you can't just bring girls in without making them audition. The others will get pissed, and we're keeping this thing together by a cunt's hair as it is!"

"Of course, she has to audition," Tawney answered. "Get Maya. She knows the routine. And get Darcy settled."

"You got it. Darcy, you can follow me to your room."

Luna sashayed away, so I turned and followed her. I caught a whiff of something that smelled like my tea-tree shampoo. I wondered if she used the same brand as me.

"Hold on," she said. She took a quick detour to open the door to what would be the garage, except it was filled with cameras, lights, and other expensive-looking pieces of equipment. "Hey Maya, we have an audition to film. Tawney told me to grab you and have you run it."

A voice from an unseen woman drifted from somewhere within the garage. "Okay. Ten minutes, I'll be ready."

Luna returned. "Ten minutes until showtime. Have you ever fucked on camera before?"

"Not knowingly."

She laughed. "Oh, I see. You got Kardashianed. Well, you'll find out soon if you're cut out for this business. Tawney probably went through some of this, but have you fucked women before?"

"Yes."

"You like it?"

"Yes."

"Good, because that's ninety-five percent of what you'll be doing. XX Cam is about women running the show from start to finish. Everyone involved is female, except for a couple of the tech people we work with sometimes, and they're so scared of us they barely qualify as men. Come on, I'll give you a tour."

She led me away from the garage down a long hallway. We stopped at the first room, which was a bedroom.

"Here's your room. You're going to be sharing with Amber. Her real name is Leslie, but we find it's easier if we just use our stage names all the time, then there's no slip-ups on camera."

"What's your stage name?"

"Luna. I don't use one. I don't give a fuck who knows what I do. Tawney found me hooking in Tijuana fifteen years ago and brought me across the border with her. I've done everything with her since then. If not for her, I'd be dead by now. I owe her my life and then some.

"Anyway, you and Amber will bunk together. She's new, but she's cool. I like her. She used to room with Mercedes until she split. Put your suitcase on that bed, but don't unpack just yet. We don't know if you're going to make it. Come on."

I stashed my suitcase by the bed to which Luna had pointed. I almost blew my cover asking if Mercedes was the name Ashleigh used here as well as on the stage in Colorado when as a new girl, I shouldn't know who Ashleigh was. I needed to be careful.

We advanced down the hall, pausing by a glass wall to our left. It looked out on a trapezoidal arboretum twenty feet wide at one end and ten at the other. It was twenty feet long and filled with palm trees and different bushes. The wide end had a door and a couple steps leading into the area.

"We shoot some outdoor stuff in there. Maya and Freya set it up so it looks like we're in a park somewhere, so we can do some crazy shit without risking getting caught. If you look at this house from the air, it looks almost like a capital letter A. This area is the center of the A. It's fun as shit. Come on."

We passed another door. "Bedroom two. Diamond and Ginger stay in there. Yes, Ginger is a redhead, but not as fit as you, or as tall, or overtly gorgeous. More freckles. She's very girl next door, but she eats pussy better than any of the other girls. If you get lonely, ask her for a favor. Come on."

We approached another room. On the outside edge of the doorframe, an LED strip ran up one side, across the top, and down the other side. The lights were green. "Now, here's the biggest thing to remember. Every room that has a light border is one of our camming rooms. If the lights are green, you're okay to enter. If it's red, a show is in session, and you cannot go in unless it's part of the act. Got it?"

"Got it." I was impressed, actually. This was a lot more organized than I had imagined. Although to be fair, I didn't know what to imagine. Luna was walking, so I scurried to catch up to her.

"Over here is the kitchen." She said it like *keetchen.* "We do a lot of meal plans and take turns with dishes and cleaning. We'll get your name in the rotation for chores. Come on."

We advanced to the rear of the house. The large room was built for hosting parties. The TV on the wall was a massive screen with a discreet projector hanging from the ceiling about halfway back. A sectional couch formed a horseshoe and looked like it could seat fifteen people comfortably. The entire back wall of the place was glass and looked out on a massive patio the entire width of the house and about forty feet deep. A swimming pool took up about two-thirds of the patio. A series of chaise lounges were scattered to the right of the pool. To the left, nearer the house, was a huge built-in hot tub. I bet it would seat ten people. A couple of café-style tables and chairs were adjacent to the jacuzzi.

Two of the three glass doors slid to the side, so the inside was almost part of the patio. Luna pulled them open, and a trio of girls, all nude, peered over at us from the chaises while we approached.

Luna pointed at them in order. "Madisin, Reesie, and April. Girls, this is Darcy. She's auditioning today."

Reesie stood up and walked over. She was all hips and ass. Well, her tits were as big as mine, but her proportions were dominated by her lower half. Like the other girls, she had a smattering of tattoos, but nothing like Tawney or Luna. She extended her hand. "Hi, Darcy! I'm Reesie. It's good to meet you. Is that your stage name?"

"No, I haven't thought of one yet."

"Oh, we have a whole list of them. We'll help you." I fought to keep my eyes from drifting to her pussy. She was waxed, but the stylist left a thin strip of hair that ended in a point right above her clitoral hood. She caught me. "It's an arrow. My regulars asked me to do it. And you have to make your regulars happy."

The sides and rear of the property were all blocked by tall hedges, effectively shielding the patio from the eyes of nosy neighbors. The back end of the patio had a transparent wall about four feet high as a barrier to prevent falling off. Luna led me over to it.

A second patio ten or so feet below us extended out twenty feet from where we stood. There was no pool, but there was a second jacuzzi and several tables and chairs scattered around. On the right side, a staircase led down to a courtyard filled with trees, bushes, and grass. It was maybe thirty feet deep, the width of the property, and completely isolated on three sides by the hedges.

Luna pointed to the patio. "Downstairs are more bedrooms, more camera rooms, the gym, and a sauna. The patio is nice for filming scenes and the lower area we call the park. Again, we do some outside shots there and make it look like we're in public. So this is the XX Cam house. What do you think?"

"It's amazing! I can't believe you guys make enough to afford this place! It must be worth millions!"

She furrowed her brow. "We make a lot of money. You don't need to worry about that yet. You need to pass your audition first."

A Goth girl walked out of the house. She wore black lipstick and had black hair down to the middle of her back, with straight bangs across her forehead, ala Bettie Paige. She wore heavy black eyeshadow and mascara that extended out from the corners of her eyes. A black t-shirt covered a slim build and smallish breasts. Her pale white legs descended from cutoff jean shorts, cropped with about a one-inch inseam. She had a pleasant smile. "Darcy? I'm Maya, the camera operator. We're ready for you inside."

Eleven

"The number one thing is to just be authentic," Tawney said. "Our fan base loves that. Try not to look at the camera during the sex part. For the regular cam shows, you'll interact with the camera all the time, but you should treat it like a regular porn for this type of video. Any questions?"

I shook my head no, but I was nervous as could be. Tawney took my hand and led me to the master bedroom. Maya had set up two big umbrella lights to illuminate the shot without letting us cast a shadow. She had a small camera on a gimble.

"Have you thought of a stage name?" Tawney asked.

"Uh, no. I haven't had a chance to figure one out yet."

"How about Ruby? It covers your hair color and the valuable gem angle."

I gave it a moment's thought. Ruby. I liked it better than Mercedes or Bugatti. It didn't seem as cliché as some of the other names I'd heard over the last few days. "Ruby is fine."

"Perfect. We'll do intros and get right into it. Just do what comes naturally. If you vapor lock, I'll take over and lead you to the promised land. Okay?"

"Vapor lock?"

"If you freeze up. It sometimes happens when girls are on camera for the first time. You'll be fine."

I glanced over at Gemma. Her face was stoic, but she gave me a wink, so I knew she was okay with what was about to happen. I kept worrying that she would get mad about the sex I would be having over the next few days, but she was convincingly playing the role of the disinterested financial detective.

"We're rolling," Maya said.

Tawney took my hand and led me to a bench at the foot of the king-sized bed. "Hi, XX Cam fans. It's Tawney, and I'm sitting here with Ruby. She's auditioning to be one of your XX Cam girls. Be sure to rate the video and let us know if you want to see more of her. Ruby, say hi to our fans."

I smiled at the camera. "Hello, everybody!"

Tawney reached out and stroked my face with the back of her tattooed left hand. "You have such soft skin," she purred, her Spanish accent making it much sexier than it should have been. She leaned over and kissed my cheek, then kissed me again a little closer to my mouth, then kissed me full on the lips. I felt tingles surge through my body, and I kissed her back.

Her hands caressed my shoulders and arms while we kissed. My skin raised goosebumps, and I felt my nipples harden. I reached up and put a hand on the side of her face, turning her head toward me more. I broke off the kiss and put my mouth on her neck, nibbling and sucking at the tender flesh.

"Mmmmm... I like that," Tawney said. I continued working on her neck and felt her lift the bottom of my shirt up. I stopped sucking on her neck and sat up straight, lifting my hands over my head so she could remove my shirt.

Her hands danced over my shoulders. She pulled one bra strap down and ran her hands over my breasts. She took a second to tweak each nipple through the fabric of my bra, pulling a sigh from me. I was vaguely aware of Maya as she moved about the room with the camera, but this tattooed Argentinian beauty had my heart beating fast already. I decided to be more aggressive.

I leaned in and kissed her again, pressing my face into hers while reaching around her back. I found the zipper in the middle of her leather top and pulled it. I felt it pop open, so I pulled it away from her, exposing her breasts. Like Luna, she was bottom-heavy, but her breasts were still bigger than mine. She had silver dollar-sized nipples that started getting hard as I slid my hands all over her torso. Her skin was soft and smooth, and I could smell jasmine and roses.

I pushed her onto the bed and fell on her, taking a nipple into my mouth and sliding a hand into her shorts. Not surprisingly, she wasn't wearing underwear. I found her pussy was wet, and I slid two fingers into her. She gasped and writhed as I worked them in and out of her.

"Fuck, Ruby, you don't mess around, do you?"

I looked up at her, still working my fingers in a steady rhythm. "If I only get one chance at this, I'm going to go for it."

I withdrew my hand, sat up, and reached my hands behind my back to undo my bra while Tawney unbuttoned my shorts and pulled them down to my knees. She buried her head in my tits, biting and sucking at my nipples. "Oh, shit! Yes!" *Was that me?*

Tawney used her leverage to spin me onto my back, and before I knew it, she had my shorts off. I grabbed the waist of her shorts and pulled, making her fall onto me. She kissed me again, hard, shoving her tongue into my mouth. She was grinding her leg against my groin, and I felt my heart beating in my clit. I was sure my panties were sopping by now.

She slid down my body, dragging her tits across mine, over my belly, and past my pussy. She slid my underwear to one side and teased my labia, tickling them, pushing them open a little, getting her fingers wet. Then she shoved them inside, hammering me repeatedly. She curled her fingers, so every thrust passed over my G-spot.

Out of the corner of my eye, I saw several figures standing just outside the bedroom entry. I didn't know we had an audience other than Gemma and Maya. It was already a turn-on getting fucked by this woman right in front of my girlfriend. It was like we were doing an extended role-playing vacation. But knowing all those people were watching made me get even hotter.

My pussy was impossibly wet. The sloshing sounds Tawney's hand was making as she attacked my pussy brought me close to the edge.

"Give me your cum," Tawney commanded. "Make this cunt explode!"

It felt like I roared. I lifted my hips off the bed and gave Tawney a shower as I squirted, soaking her and the bed. She pulled her hand out and slapped it on my pussy several times, spattering my cum all over my thighs and belly. I was shocked at the feeling of her hitting my clit like that. It both hurt and felt incredible. I cried out as I came again, though I didn't squirt this time.

She grabbed my panties by the waistband and pulled them off. I lifted my hips to help her, then she slid her fingers back into me, this time sliding two fingers from her other hand into my ass as well. Tawney alternated them, sliding into my pussy and out of my ass, and vise-versa, over and over.

I was moaning and crying out and speaking in tongues. My pelvic muscles were contracting again and again, my orgasm lasting an eternity. I never wanted her to stop. "More!" I screamed. "More, more, more, fuck me! Oh, shit!" I squirted again. How did I have that much fluid in my body?

Tawney withdrew her hands, but my pussy and ass were vibrating so hard that I kept cumming, my pelvic muscles contracting and pushing fluid out on the already soaked bed. I lifted my head high enough to see that Maya was filming over Tawney's shoulders, probably zoomed in on my hole as it contracted and relaxed while I came. I let my legs fall all the way open and laid my head back on the bed. I was spent.

"Cut!" Tawney called out. "Ruby, that was awesome. The way you just collapsed at the end... people are going to be jacking and jilling it to this one big time." She stroked my thigh, sending shivers through my pelvis. "Take your time collecting yourself. You did great."

I shut my eyes and stayed where I was, catching my breath. My legs had stopped functioning. In the hallway, the girls all applauded. I looked over, and all of them—Madisin, Reesie, April, Luna, and Gemma were clapping.

I smiled. Step one was complete: prove to the girls that I belong here, that I'm one of them.

"You can go unpack your suitcase when you're ready," Luna said as she laid a light blanket over me. "I don't need to see the reactions to the video. You're not going anywhere."

Twelve

I lay on the bed for a few minutes, quietly processing what had just happened. Twice before I had sex acts captured on video—without my knowledge—and posted to the internet. But those were small-time, one-off videos with no real following, and one of them was ten years ago when all this cam and sex-site stuff hadn't really taken off yet.

This video was different. A clip would be posted on the big porn sites, with the full video posted on the XX Cam members-only site. My face, body, everything I had would be on the internet for anyone to see. And it would be compensated, so I was now an official sex worker, or as the uptight crowd would call me, a pornographer. I knew this was temporary, but I never expected to find myself in this position! But, at the same time, growing up, I never expected to be in a gang-bang, love fucking women, or do a lot of the other things I've done.

And damn, what Tawney just did to me felt fantastic.

"Are you going to be okay?"

I was startled by the voice. My eyes popped open to find Maya still in the room, taking down the equipment. I got a really good look at her for the first time. I was never all that into the Goth look, but Maya was pretty. "Yeah, I'm fine, Maya. Just reveling in the bliss for a minute."

"That was really, really hot, Ruby. Tawney wasn't kidding. After I master the sound and clean it up, in thirty minutes or so, people around the world are going to be masturbating to you. I bet you hit a half million views by midnight."

I sat up, the enormous wet spot under me now cold against my skin. I looked around for my clothes, suddenly aware that I was fully nude in front of this woman while we had a casual conversation. "You think so? I was, um, *Kardashianed* in a video, and it has like a quarter-million views. But that was over the last few months."

"Oh, shit yeah. By the time I get it posted, it will be..." her eyes rolled up while she did the math in her head, "seven PM on the east coast, midnight, one AM in Europe. Prime masturbation times."

I laughed. "Is there any time that people won't do it?"

"Haha! No. Twenty-four by seven, people are tugging on their junk."

I wanted to learn more about her, so I pressed forward. "Do you do it? Be a Camgirl, I mean, not masturbate. I assume you do that."

96

She smiled. "I edit these videos and sit in damp panties all day long. Yeah, I masturbate, or Freya takes care of me."

"Who's Freya? I don't think I've met her."

"She's out with Amber, Diamond, and Ginger doing some remotes. That's remote shoots. You'll probably have to do that next. Anyway, she and I do all the camera work and editing of the videos we post." Her mouth spread into a big grin. "We work in the nude a lot, and we fuck all the time. But that's for us, not for the cameras. I've never been on the other side of the lens."

"Do you want to?"

She pondered it for a moment. "Sometimes yes, and sometimes no. I worry about what my mom would think when she found out. And, trust me, they always find out."

I hadn't thought about that. It was too late now; I was in all the way. I just had to hope no one would ever send a link to my dad and say, *"Hey, Bob, isn't this your girl?"*

I found my underwear on the floor, and they were as wet as if they'd come out of the wash. I would not be putting them back on. My shorts were next to them, and my shirt and bra were on the bench at the end of the bed where Tawney and I started out. "So, if you aren't on camera, what drew you here? To XX Cam, I mean. We are in

Hollywood, after all. I'm sure there are similar jobs with the studios."

"Honestly? Tawney pays us about two and a half times what we would make at one of the studios. And XX Cam has a healthcare plan that doesn't cost us any more than what we'd get through the unions. And we love it here! You saw that view. This place is paradise. I hope Tawney figures out the money stuff. I don't want to lose this place."

I played dumb. "What money stuff?"

"Someone has been hacking our bank accounts. That's what that black-haired goddess is doing here. She's some sort of detective or something, though, with a body like hers, she should get in front of the camera."

I smiled internally at Maya drooling over my woman. "Well, maybe Tawney will convince her. Are you worried this whole thing will get shut down?"

"A little. Some of the girls think it's Tawney doing it, so there's some fractures happening amongst them. A couple of them have left already; that's why you're here."

"Who thinks it's Tawney?"

"You know, it's not really my place to say. Talk to the girls. You'll figure it out."

I took that as all she had to say on the matter, so I changed my tack. "Do you need some help with this stuff?"

"No, I've got it. You should go get to know the other girls. You'll be working *very* closely with them."

I ditched my clothes on the bed in my room. I debated opening my suitcase and retrieving fresh panties, but all the women around here were nude, so I figured I'd meet them on their terms. I shut the door and walked out to the patio. I felt a tingle in my groin as I crossed the threshold. I had been back in California for about four hours, and I'd already gotten laid, and I was walking outdoors, nude.

It was a hot afternoon in LA, the temperature hitting ninety-six while we were at the In-N-Out burger. It was only a couple of degrees cooler up here in the canyon, and the late afternoon sun wasn't letting the temperature drop.

The patio faced almost due south, so the sun was drifting toward the horizon to our right. Soon the hedges would cast a shadow over half of the patio. Luna and Reesie were the only women out there.

Luna sat in a chaise with a portable desk straddling her. She was paying attention to a laptop with some sort of video playing on the screen. She seemed very focused, so I didn't bother her. Reesie saw me and got out of her chair.

"Ruby! Welcome to the team!" She trotted over and gave me a hug, not caring that we were both naked. I stared at the arrow of pubic hair that pointed to her vagina as she approached and felt the tickle of her patch against me as she pulled me tight to her. Her skin was hot from lying in the sun, and it felt good pressed against me. She looked at Luna. "She's moderating a show right now. Come on, I want to show you something."

She grabbed my pinky and tugged, leading me over to the four-foot plastic wall. Reesie was built much like Luna and Tawney. Her tits were smaller than Luna's but close to the same as Tawney's. The three of them all had wide hips and voluptuous asses. She oozed sex. As I walked, I felt my pussy get wet. *Jesus, I think you're going to be soaked the entire time we're here!* My brain, as usual, was being helpful.

We stopped at the thick plastic half wall. Reesie gestured at the city down below us at the foot of the canyon. "That's West Hollywood. Do you know the Whisky A Go-Go?"

"I've heard of it. Never been there."

"Well, it's right down there." She pointed, but I had no idea what she was pointing at. "And you know about Tinder, right?" I nodded yes. "Well, they have an office right by Whisky A Go-Go, but I think you have to be, like, a computer coder to work there. And the Roxy is right over there." She moved her hand to the west a few blocks, but I still had no idea what building she was pointing at. It was still pretty cool to be in a spot so close to these well-known Hollywood fixtures, though.

Reesie waved her arm back and forth. "And of course, that road is Sunset Boulevard." She pointed to the west. "If you go around that bend a ways you get to Beverly Hills and the famous Rodeo Drive. We like to do some of our remotes there."

"It's gorgeous up here. And it feels so decadent to be naked outdoors. I could never do this at home."

"I know, right? Every now and then, the gardeners come through, and we give them a little show, but unless you're in a plane or inside the hedge, you can't see what we're doing. I hope Gemma can figure out what's happening with the money. It would suck trying to get a new place set up for us."

I was a little taken aback at the mention of Gemma's name, but then I remembered that Reesie was the one who introduced Gemma to Tawney all those years ago, so of course she'd know her real name. "Yeah, that would suck. Maya told me a little about what's going on. She said some of the girls think Tawney is behind it?"

Reesie's head swiveled around, her eyes searching for anyone close enough to hear us. "You put that out of your mind right now and don't let anyone else ever hear you say that. The last person it would ever be is Tawney. She's pulled money from her personal safe deposit box to pay these girls, especially Maya and Freya since they keep the content flowing on our member's only site. They shouldn't be repeating that kind of stuff, especially to anyone new."

"I'm sorry, I didn't mean anything by it. I'm just glad to have this shot."

She reached out and ran her hand up and down my upper arm, stroking it affectionately. "Of course, you didn't, sweetie. You just didn't know better. How could you? You've been here for what, an hour? If you hear any of the girls spreading rumors like that, you let me or Luna know right away, okay? We need to put a stop to that shit as soon as it happens."

"Okay. But since you brought it up, why does Tawney have a safe deposit box? I don't know anyone who has one of those anymore."

Reesie studied me for a minute. I assumed she was assessing whether or not she could trust me and how much to tell me in either case. "Well, there's a couple of reasons. One, she wants to have cash stashed if she ever needs it. I think it's an artifact of growing up in Argentina, and it turns out was smart in our case, and two, she's started pulling money out the same day it hits the account so it can't get stolen. It's a huge pain in the ass, but it's helped keep us intact for the time being. So, don't worry, when your time comes, you'll get paid."

I decided that was enough of my questions for now. I didn't want to make Reesie suspicious of me. I nodded at the pool. "So tell me, how's the pool and hot tub?"

"Oh, the pool is to die for. We keep it at eighty-eight degrees year-round so you can swim in the winter. It's delightful. It's salt water, so it won't jack with your hair coloring."

"Oh, this is my natural color."

"Shut *up*! It can't be—it's such a unique red!" She let her eyes drift down to my thatch of pubic hair and smiled.

"It's burgundy. I used to hate it when I was a kid, and was all gangly and awkward. I tried coloring it blonde in college, but that was a disaster. Now I'm just as awkward, but I love the color now."

"Well, I love it too. And I don't believe you were *ever* gangly or awkward." She looked at my naked body, giving me shivers of pleasure. "You're dressed for it. Come on, let's get in."

We waded into the pool. It felt fantastic. It was hard for me to believe, but other than a trip to the mountains a few months ago, I've not been naked in any body of water other than my tub. Like walking through the threshold of this house onto the patio without clothing, laying on my back and lazily drifting across the pool felt erotic. The warm water flowed unfettered over my breasts and across my vagina without the interference of a bikini. I loved every second of it. I had a flash thought of pleasuring myself, but I didn't feel entirely comfortable enough to rub one out with Reesie floating just a few feet away.

I had been in exactly one video, which hadn't aired yet, and I was already loving this lifestyle. I could see why Gemma warned me about it.

Reesie and I lazily floated in the pool for fifteen minutes. I was thinking about getting out when she bumped into me. She startled me, and I exclaimed, "Ooh!"

"Oh, sorry, Ruby! I didn't mean to scare you." She touched my shoulders. I put my feet down and turned to find her facing me, mere inches away. She was gorgeous, and her wet hair slicked back gave her an added layer of appeal. We both bobbed, crouching, in the four and a half feet of water. I don't know if the motion of the water moved me, or if I did it subconsciously, but suddenly our bodies touched, first our breasts and then our stomachs. She slid a leg over mine, and our pussies made contact. I gasped, and Reesie started running her hands up and down my sides and over my buttocks. I was frozen. I just stared into her pale blue eyes and wondered if she would make me cum.

Reesie licked her lips, and I leaned in and kissed her. I was timid at first, but she opened her mouth and encouraged me to be more forceful. Our tongues twisted around each other, and she moaned as I bit and pulled on her lower lip.

She walked me over to the edge of the pool and pressed me against the tile wall. I gasped as her hand found my slit, and she dragged her fingers through it, past my clit. Reflexively, I spread my legs apart to give her more access. I was waving her in. She pushed two fingers through my folds, and I rolled my head back onto the concrete lip of the pool. With my head supported by the wall, my body buoyed up, and Reesie moved her hands under my ass and lifted, bringing my pussy to her face. *Fuck yes!* My brain screamed. For once, I was in violent agreement with it.

Reesie kissed my clit. "You have a beautiful twat," she complimented me. "People are going to go crazy for this."

I wondered what the appropriate response was, but before I could formulate an answer, she pierced my beautiful twat with her tongue, pushing it between my lips and as far into my depths as she could. The only thing I seemed capable of saying was, "Oh, fuuuuck!"

My hips bucked in the water, and Reesie pulled me tighter against her face. I hooked my legs over her shoulders and gave complete control of my body over to her.

And then she released me. My legs dropped back into the water, and I was suddenly facing her again.

"Oh, Ruby, the things I'm going to do to you. Hold onto this feeling... you're going to be a guest on my show tonight after dinner. You'd better hydrate."

She turned and waded to the steps, climbing out and returning to her chaise, where she laid and drip-dried in the sun.

It took me a minute to recover myself. After Tawney ravished me earlier, I hadn't really come down completely. Wandering around naked had kept my libido at a fast idle. Then things between Reesie and I had started so unexpectedly, I was swept away by the lusty feelings that being nude in the pool had brought bubbling to the surface. Now I had to downshift and regain my composure.

We could get used to this life. Fuck yeah, we could, Brain. Fuck yeah.

Thirteen

After I regained my composure in the pool, I went inside and unpacked my suitcase. I fought back the overwhelming urge to masturbate. I knew if I did, I wouldn't have the same level of passion for the show tonight. My first show—and you never get a second chance to make a good first impression, so I wanted to go into it with a full libido, rife with the angst that Reesie had left me with.

As the newest girl in the house, I was on dish duty after dinner. April and Maya cooked, and I helped Luna set the table.

While I leaned across the table, placing forks next to the plates she was setting out, Luna gave me the once-over. "You look like you keep yourself in good shape. We keep a pretty strict diet here. You're welcome to eat whatever you want, but you're going keto if you eat with the group. We don't have much in the way of carbs in the house."

I smiled. "I've not kept strict keto, but close. Bacon and eggs are my favorite breakfast! When I cheat, it's with alcohol. Wine or tequila, mostly."

"What, in margaritas, or straight?"

"Margaritas, actually."

She squinted at me. "There's a lot of sugar in the mix in those. You might as well be drinking soda." She stopped herself. "Sorry, you're an adult, and whatever you're doing is working. I don't mean to nag. Some of the girls are pretty young and don't know better."

"That's okay. It helps to have someone watching out for you. You don't want a moment of weakness to become a habit."

She smiled. "Exactly."

Counting Gemma and myself, there were twelve women in the house to cook for. Amber, Diamond, and Freya weren't back from their remote shoot yet, and Madisin was hosting a show. So, after the rest of us ate our zucchini pasta with chicken and pistachios with a cauliflower risotto on the side, I packed four leftover meals in glass food storage containers for the missing women and put them in the fridge. I washed the pots, loaded the dishwasher, turned it on, and went to my room.

I showered and washed my hair, setting it with light curls. I didn't want to get washed out in the lights Reesie was sure to have set up with my fair complexion, so I actually applied more makeup than usual, opting for a more smokey eye and more color in the cheeks. Luna told me to wear something casual but to be sure to include a bra and underwear. She said the more things I had to take off, the more tips we could wring out of the viewers. Once I was dressed, she wanted me to come out for a quick tutorial on what would happen during the show.

She showed me the interface for the chat room. She would moderate for us—meaning she would take care of any trolls, exhort people for tips, and so on. She'd set the limits for the action, too. No clothes come off until we hit ten thousand tokens in tips—which she explained is the equivalent of five hundred dollars. She said at that point, every thousand tokens, more clothes will come off, or we will make out, or whatever Reesie decides the goals will be. Once we hit twenty thousand, we'll do a 'ticket show' – where people pay a set amount of tokens for access to a private show. People could also purchase VIP access, granting them discounted admission to the ticket show both this night and going forward.

"Also," Luna said, "there will be bidding for your panties and bra, so wear something you don't mind getting rid of."

"Okay... I guess I'm not super attached to what I have on."

"Now, here's the conceit for tonight's show. Reesie came up with it while she was eating you out in the pool."

I kind of loved how casually she said that. It also made my pussy tingle, both from hearing it said in such a matter-of-fact style, but also because it made me remember how it felt, bobbing in the water, giving myself over to Reesie. Luna was still talking, so I forced the thoughts from my mind.

"We've teased a couple of three-second clips of your audition on our Snap channel to generate some buzz about our newest cam girl. The response has been great. So, for Reesie's show, we're billing it as a one-night-only affair while you wait to find out if you're in or not. She's going to tell her audience that you don't know you're on camera—that you think Reesie's just watching a movie. You'll sit next to her, and while the tips accumulate, she'll chat with you. You'll see a blue light flash on the wall opposite where you sit whenever we hit one of the thresholds. Just follow Reesie's lead.

"Once the action starts, do what comes naturally, just like in the pool. We have a couple of cameras we'll switch between, so Reesie may reposition herself or move your leg or something like that, so we have the best camera angle. We have audio signals for the camera switches, but you don't need to worry about that. And, once we hit the token threshold, we'll go to a private show. While we sell tickets, she'll talk to you about and spill the secret that you just fucked on camera. Act mad for a second, then ask her to see the chat room. You'll interact with the fans for a few minutes, and once we get one thousand in ticket sales, we'll up the price for a few minutes, start the show, and then when it's over, you can just chat with the folks for a while, and they'll tip you more. I know it's a lot to take in. Just let Reesie guide you. Okay?"

I nodded. "Okay. Is there anything I *shouldn't* do?"

"The main thing is do not *ever* give away our location. People know we're in California, but that's as specific as we've ever gotten. The other thing is never do anything for free. It can be tempting, especially on nights when tips are slow, to try something to get them going again. Don't. Make them tip. I don't mean to make it sound like we're taking advantage of our viewers. They're mostly super sweet people who come here for the nudity, but they stay with XX Cam girls because of the relationships they build. But, we are running a business too. They understand that."

"Okay, no location, no freebies. Got it."

"Are you nervous?"

"No," I lied. "Well, yes, actually. I'm really fucking nervous."

"Ruby, just do what you did in the audition today. People will be crazy wanting more of you. We're going to tell them we can't bring you onboard until we have a hundred new subscribers to our premium channel, and we'll get your shows slotted when we have five hundred new ones. Until then, you'll do some remotes and such for the subscribers, so we have some content built up and in reserve."

"How much are the premium memberships?"

"Ten dollars per month."

"So, you're going to make five thousand dollars before I do one show?"

"No, *we* will make twenty-five hundred; *you* will make twenty-five hundred. XX Cam gets fifty percent of your take. That covers the rent, the food, utilities, all that stuff."

"Wow, you guys have really thought this through."

"It was Gemma, the woman who's here investigating the financial issues. She put together the business model. We've made some modifications over the last few years since she left and some things like Snap came into the picture, but she's the one who put XX Cam on the map."

"Wow! She must be pretty smart then. I hope she can help us."

"She will. I'm just glad to have someone here who gives a shit about finding out who's doing it."

I nodded for a second. "Who do you think it is? Do you think it's an inside job?"

Like Reesie and Maya before her, Luna studied me for a minute and decided she could trust me. "You know, at first, I did. I thought maybe it was Mercedes. In fact, when she quit and went back home with Gino and his crew, I was sure of it. But then I heard she's stripping again, which doesn't make sense if she made off with several hundred grand. So now I don't know."

"Who's Gino?" I played dumb. I knew Gino was Little Chub, but again, I wasn't supposed to have that knowledge.

"Oh, sorry. Gino owns a strip club in Colorado. He was out here for some business deal a couple of months ago and came to a party we hosted. I guess Mercedes had been in contact with him and invited him. She used to work there years and years ago. But it seems odd to steal that much money only to go back on the pole."

"Well, we'll know soon enough, I guess."

Luna nodded and took a drink of her water. "I hope so." She looked at the laptop screen. "Okay, Ruby. You're on."

Fourteen

The office door was what designers called a 'barn door,' but was really a sliding wall that locked in place from the inside, so once Tawney secured it, no one could get in. She wore a black bra and matching panties, and Gemma ogled her as she walked back into the bedroom.

"You look just as good as you did the last time I saw you."

Tawney smiled. "Thank you, love. You look better than before. You've been working out to impress the *pelirroja*."

"It does impress my red-head, yes, but I don't do it for her. You know me better than that."

"Yes," Tawney purred through her Spanish accent. "She's something, though. Did you see the way she came after me today?"

"I was standing right there, watching you put her in her place."

Tawney stuck out her breasts and arched her back. "You're damn right I did! There's only one alpha in this house!"

Gemma patted the bed. "Alright, get your alpha ass over here and turn this thing on."

Tawney hopped onto the bed and sat next to Gemma, leaning back against the Bed Buddy bean bag chairs that allowed them to sit up while in bed. She took a lap desk from Gemma and pressed a couple of buttons on a remote. A sixty-five-inch LED TV descended from the ceiling and turned on, first displaying a blue screen, then a beautiful mountain meadow with a stream running through it. It was a computer login screen, and Tawney sat the remote down and began typing on a keyboard.

The TV changed again, showing the desktop for Windows. Tawney opened a browser, then logged into the chat-cam site that hosted their shows. She found Reesie's show already in progress.

Over the video window, the show title read:

NEW XX CAM GIRL DOESN'T KNOW THIS IS A SHOW. SEDUCTION COMMENCES AT GOAL. [10000 TOKENS REMAINING]

Reesie was sitting on a couch wearing a pair of mid-length running shorts, socks that covered her calves, and a baby doll t-shirt that left four inches of her stomach exposed. She was looking at the camera and talking to her fans.

"...sexiest audition I've ever seen, and you all know I've seen a lot of them. So, I'm sure you all are going to vote her in, but until then, we're letting

her stay with us. So tomorrow, you're going to want to cast your vote to let her stay or make her go. But only our members can vote, so go sign up at our website."

In the chat sidebar, user name *XXluna*, Luna's moderator handle, posted the web address. Different chat members were sending messages, and a moderator message popped up:

> NOTICE: THE FORMAT OF TONIGHT'S SHOW: COUNTDOWN TO GOAL. NO PVT NO C2C. NO PC.

Gemma knew the shorthand. No private shows, camera to camera connections, no personal chats.

Reesie continued her introduction.

"So tonight, we're doing a special show. I was in the pool earlier with the new girl, her name is Ruby, and... well, things got a little physical. She was giving herself over to me, and I was about to go for it. Then I thought,... you know who would love to see this? All the Reesie Love fans out there."

Tawney opened another tab and logged into the social media management tool. She scheduled tweets to be posted every ten minutes for two hours, telling their two hundred thousand followers to go watch the crazy show Reesie Love was putting on. She switched back to the video tab.

"So, right as I almost had her ready to cum, I walked away and told her I forgot I had to do something, but I wanted to hook up with her later. I talked to the other girls, and they've got my back on this. They're going to send her in here in a few minutes, and I'm going to go dark. I'm going to act like I'm watching a show, but you guys will all see Ruby and me the whole time. I know she's dying to pick it back up where we left off, but you have to get us to the goal to make it happen!

"Once we hit our second goal, and I get her off, we'll do a ticket show, and I'll see if we can introduce her to the Lush or the Domi and let you guys have some fun with her. Okay, she's going to come in here in a couple of minutes. Start tipping now, guys. The faster we hit that goal, the faster we can all see what she's made of!"

"Hey Tawney, won't the site bust your balls for having Darcy—"

"Ruby," Tawney corrected.

"Right, Ruby. For having her on cam without being verified by them first?"

"Luna's submitting proof of age and all that stuff for her. If they notice – and that's a big if, we'll get a slap, but if we get it squared right away, it's no big deal. We bring in a lot of tokens for them, so they cut us a lot of slack. Has she ever used the Lush or Domi?" Tawney asked, referring to the interactive vibrators that the viewers control with their tips.

Gemma shook her head. "No."

"Oh, my. The Lush is going to blow her away! Are you going to be okay with this?"

Gemma smiled. "Yeah, I'll be fine. But Dar— er, Ruby, she's in a whole new world now. This is going to get very interesting."

Fifteen

I approached the door with the red LED lights around the frame. I paused with my hand hovering over the handle. Was I ready for this? If I walked through that door, there was no going back. I'd be on camera, hundreds of people—maybe over a thousand, Luna said—watching me get seduced by Reesie.

In for a penny, in for a pound. That wasn't the first time I'd heard that from my brain. And she was right. I turned the knob and stepped into the room.

Reesie was on the couch innocently watching the TV. Her face lit up when I walked in. "Hey, Ruby! Did you finally get done with all the dishes?"

I smiled back. I could see the cameras in the room, the umbrella lamps, the signal lights. I took it all in right away without trying to look at any one specific thing, then focused my gaze on Reesie. "Yeah, I did. How long do I get to do that?"

She gave me a devilish smile. "Until we get another new girl. But, I saved you a seat!" She patted the cushion next to her.

I sat down and tucked my feet under me, leaning away from her. I figured the extra effort to pull me into her clutches would play well on camera. "What are we watching?"

"I was just surfing. Do you like Supernatural? I could put that on."

"I *love* that show. I was just rewatching it before I moved out here." It's true, I was. I liked having it on in the background while I worked.

"Cool." Reesie put the show on but left the volume down so it wouldn't drown out our conversation. I knew out in the living room, Luna was moderating the chat and urging people to get us to the tip limit so we could get into some action.

"So, what do you think of the house so far?" She reached down and touched my foot, squeezing it gently.

"It's super nice. And everyone has been awesome so far. Especially you." I shifted positions to allow her to grab my whole foot, not just the outer edge. "That feels nice."

"Stretch out and let me see your feet." Reesie reached over the edge of the couch and procured a bottle of lotion.

"What are you doing with that?"

"Just relax." She squirted some of the viscous fluid into her palm and dropped the bottle to the floor. She rubbed her hands together to warm it up, then grabbed my right foot. With the lotion spread all over the sole, she pressed her thumbs into the bottom of my foot, starting at the heel and sliding them to the toes, each of which she grabbed individually, squeezing them and tugging them. Then she repeated the process.

"Oh, god, that feels nice." I closed my eyes and slowly moved my pelvis in a circle, moaning the entire time. After several passes from heel to toes, Reesie moved to the other foot. I rolled my head toward the camera and licked my lips. "Oh, Reesie, you're hired. You can be my personal masseuse."

"Mmmmm... does that mean I get to rub and touch you all over?"

I smiled. "I was letting you do that this afternoon."

She stole a glance at the camera and recapped the story for the viewers. "You mean in the pool?"

"Yes, in the pool. What was that? Were you just trying to edge me? Because, fuck, I've been super sensitive ever since."

"I just didn't want to go too far until we got to know each other better." She put my left foot on the floor, opening my legs, and grabbed the bottle again. With more lotion on her hands, she began squeezing and massaging my right calf, holding my leg up in the air. "Your legs are really toned, Ruby. You must work out a lot." She slid her hand past my knee and up my thigh, stopping short of my groin.

I let out a gasp, and it wasn't acting. "Uh, yeah, I do workout, um, a lot. Are you trying to turn me on?"

"Is it working?"

"What do you think? I haven't stopped thinking about the pool all evening."

She sat my leg on the couch and pulled the right one up, laying my ankle on her shoulder and working on my left calf like she did the right. "I like touching you. Your skin is so soft."

"Mmmmmm." It was all I could say.

She pressed her thumbs into the back of my knee. Only Gemma had found that spot. There's apparently a nerve that connects that spot directly with my pussy, because it tingles, and I get wet the second someone focuses attention there. I moaned and involuntarily moved a hand to my crotch, rubbing my pussy through my shorts.

Reesie laid my leg down. "Okay, now do me!"

I sat up on my elbows and looked at her. She tossed the lotion to me and laid down on the couch, stretching out and laying her long legs on me.

I sat all the way up and squirted some lotion on my hand, warming it like she did. "Flip over," I directed her. She obliged and lay on her stomach, her nice big butt facing up.

I kneeled on the couch, lining up my knees just below hers, and making her spread her legs

123

around me. I bent her right leg so her foot was sticking up in the air and began kneading the sole, pressing my thumbs into the arches making swirling motions.

"Oh my god, that feels amazing!" She sounded breathy like she was getting hot herself. I worked on her calf for a couple of minutes, then switched to her left foot and calf.

I scooted closer to her on the couch, my knees now a third of the way up her thighs, and squirted the lotion directly on the backs of her legs. She squealed for a second, but then I started rubbing them, pressing the heel of my palms into each leg and sliding them toward the bottom of her butt cheeks. I worked closer and closer, forcing her legs to open wider until my hands disappeared into her shorts.

Now it was her turn to gasp. She turned her head toward me and said, "Ooh, you're being bad!"

I reached out and put my hand on the right side of her face, holding it where it was, and I leaned in and kissed her, taking her lower lip into my mouth and pulling it as I backed away.

On the wall above the TV, a blue LED lit up. We'd hit the first goal, ten thousand tokens. We were now clear to get more physical.

Reesie saw the light too. "Oh, Ruby, now it's my turn."

Sixteen

In the master bedroom, Tawney was laughing. The chat had blown through the first goal before the girls had really done anything. "Holy shit, Gemma. People really want to watch them fuck. I can't think of the last time I saw so much money come through so quickly."

"Luna's doing a great job moderating too. You guys have really got this down to a science now."

"Yeah, the girls have really stepped up. Moderating for each other, filming and editing videos, working out every day. They're really committed to making a quality product. That's why I can't believe any of them would be stealing from the rest."

Darcy and Reesie were making out onscreen, and Reesie was pulling Darcy's shirt over her head. She stopped, leaning in to kiss her again while her arms were trapped in the shirt.

In the chat sidebar, tips were still rolling in. People were crazy for this show. "It's hard to tell from their user IDs, but it looks like there are more women than men in here," Gemma observed.

"That's pretty typical." She clicked on the contest stats. The room was the number one active cam with almost two thousand registered users watching and nearly thirteen thousand in total. "Those are big numbers. Our shows hit number one all the time and almost always are in the top ten. But they're five thousand viewers over the next cam."

"And they haven't even gotten physical yet," Gemma said.

Tawney slid her leg over Gemma's. "Speaking of getting physical, did Dar—I mean, Ruby—give you a hall pass too?"

Gemma put a hand on Tawney's thigh and ran it up and down. "I told her that something would probably happen between you and me. That, given our history, the other girls would think it was weird if it didn't."

A sly grin spread across Tawney's face. "Well, this night just got a whole lot more interesting."

Gemma kissed Tawney's shoulder. "Are you going to do to me what you did to Ruby?"

"Hell, no, bitch, you're going to do that to me! And then yes, I'll take care of you. I need to take advantage of this arrangement while I can!"

Gemma pushed her over and climbed on top of her, the action on-screen forgotten for the moment.

Seventeen

Reesie sat up, taking my hands and pulling me close to her. "I was so jealous when I watched your audition today, Ruby. All I could think was that I wished it was me in that bedroom with you instead of Tawney."

"But you could have had me in the pool. Why didn't you take me then?"

She shrugged. "I told you, I had some things to take care of. I wanted to make sure my evening was free for you."

"Well, I'm not disappointed. I mean, this is pretty great."

Reesie held my gaze for a long second before she grabbed the remote and pressed a few buttons. The show on the TV disappeared, replaced by sensual electronic dance music with a hypnotic beat. I could feel my head bob involuntarily as I started to succumb to the rhythm. Reesie took my hands and pulled me closer to her. She released her grip and dropped my hands to her waist. I grabbed a handful of her shirt, pulling it to keep me close to her, while she leaned forward and gave me a long, tongue-filled kiss. Her mouth was minty and wet. She explored my mouth, her tongue seeking every curve and nuance of my teeth, tongue, and gums. I was glad I took a mint when Luna offered me one before the show. I made a mental note to keep mints handy while I was undercover here.

Reesie shifted positions, getting to her knees on the couch and looming over me, still kissing me. She tugged at my shirt, and I surrendered my arms to her so she could pull the garment off me. I wore a purple and black bra, and contrary to what I had told Luna earlier, it was one of my favorites. If someone was going to buy it, I'd part with it for the sake of my ruse, but I would have to order another one right away.

I laid back on the couch, pulling Reesie on top of me. She began kissing my neck, and I felt warmth flow through me. It was getting real now.

I wondered how many people were watching us. I know Reesie had over one hundred forty thousand followers, but only a fraction would be watching. Would it be five hundred? A thousand? More? As she unbuttoned my shorts and pulled them down past my knees, I felt a moment of panic that potentially thousands of people were watching a woman undress me. The panic was replaced by adrenaline as she began kissing my stomach and dragging her nails over my ribs. A flood of warmth surged through my pussy.

I realized my back was arched, and I was breathing hard, my stomach rising and falling rapidly with each gasp. Reesie put my left leg on the floor and raised my right one, I assumed, to give the viewers a better view when she started rubbing me over my panties. Her lips peppered my thigh with kisses. Damn, this woman was getting me hot.

She straddled my right leg, leaving the camera a good view of my crotch as she rubbed her leg against me. I was wet and knew that the viewers would get a direct look at the damp spot on my panties when she moved her leg. I supposed that would drive up the price in the auction.

Her hand wiggled its way inside my underwear, her fingers teasing my clit while her leg ground into my labia. I opened my legs wider, gasping for air as Reesie leaned over me, and her mouth found the hollow above my collar bone and explored it with her tongue, licking and kissing her way up my neck to my ear. "You're so fucking hot!" she hissed. I didn't know if the mic was strong enough to pick that up, but I heard it plain enough. I writhed underneath her, moaning.

Her free hand moved my bra strap out of the way so she could kiss along my shoulder. As she ran her fingers down my arm, she hooked the strap and pulled it down, loosening the cup around my breast. With gravity's assist, my nipple made its first appearance of the night. Reesie's lips found it immediately, pulling a gasp out of me while she sucked on it until it was hard in her mouth.

I sat up and reached behind my back, fussing with the clasp on my bra for a few seconds, then slid my arms out of the straps and tossed it aside. I dropped back to the couch, and Reesie fell upon the other breast like a hungry animal. I wanted to say something hot and sexy, but all I could muster was, "Oh, fuck!"

She moved her leg and slid a finger inside my pussy while she sucked on my nipples. My hips bucked, and I moaned again.

Finally, Reesie hooked the waistband of my panties and pulled, my eager hips lifting and giving her an assist in getting them off. She ran her hands up the inside of my thighs, making me shudder. I re-opened my legs to her, dropping my left foot to the floor, so the viewers had a good view of my pussy as Reesie slid two fingers inside me and began working my G-spot. That pulled another "Oh fuck!" out of me, and my hips started to spasm.

She brought her mouth to my belly and kissed a trail south. When she reached my clit, she hovered over it, blowing softly on it with cool breath, then dancing over it with her tongue. The sudden temperature change made her touch more intense. I cried out and grabbed onto the sides of the couch cushion while my hips thrust themselves at her.

Her fingers stayed inside me, her hand riding my vagina like a cowboy would ride a bull. She put her mouth on me, and I couldn't focus on anything but her. She had her head at an angle, sliding her tongue through my slit like a credit card, then flicked it over my engorged clit. She kissed and sucked it like she was making out with my pussy.

Her left hand was caressing my chest, pinching my nipples. Her right hand was pounding against my pussy, the fingers sliding in and out. She made the 'come here' motion to work my G-spot while her mouth and tongue massaged my labia and clit. I was in heaven. My mission to find information on who was stealing the money from the XXCam account was forgotten. Gemma sharing a bed with, and probably fucking, Tawney was forgotten. All my world was in the sensations of Reesie Love having her way with my body, fucking me on camera.

The camera! I realized my most private, intimate moment was being broadcast, live over the internet to potentially thousands of people. It wasn't the first time I had been filmed having sex, but it was the first time it was in real-time. Men and women all over the world were watching me get eaten out by the voluptuous woman, watching her put her fingers inside me. They might even be touching themselves right now. In fact, I hoped they were. I hoped they were lost in the throes of passionate self-care, fantasizing that it was *their* mouth devouring my cunt, or that it was *my pussy* sliding up and down their cock instead of their hand. I wanted to feel the psychic energy of ten thousand simultaneous orgasms.

"Fuck, Reesie, I'm going to cum, I'm at the edge, I'm going to fall off, oh, my god!" I screamed out, letting the audience know this was it. And it was. The pressure on my G-spot was the trigger, and my contractions shot my cum out all over Reesie's arm, the splash getting her pants and shirt wet as well. Contraction after contraction, I came forever, my breath coming in rapid gasps. Reesie kept fingering me, kept licking me, prolonging my orgasm, torturing me, holding me under the wave that kept crashing down on me, hammering, animating my pelvis.

My limbs finally went limp. I lay there, legs spread, left arm hanging loose off the couch, right arm resting against the cushioned back. I licked my lips and opened my eyes, looking at Reesie. She beamed like a champion who just won a race.

"Holy shit Ruby, you just came so hard you almost made *me* cum!"

"Yeah. Wow. That was worth the wait." I let my hand drift down to my vagina, feeling the wetness that was spread all over my mound, my inner thighs, everywhere. I sighed, letting my legs stay open for another couple of seconds before pushing myself into a sitting position, leaning back against the arm of the couch. I lifted my left foot and put it on Reesie's leg, stroking it from knee to hip.

"I have a confession to make, Ruby." Reesie was suddenly serious.

"That's never a good thing. Well, tell me now while I'm still too weak to get mad."

"You know how you auditioned for a spot as an XX Cam girl today?"

I laughed. "Yeah, I do remember that audition. It's hard to forget a heavily tattooed Argentinian goddess ravishing you and leaving you like a wet rag on her bed. So, yeah, I remember that."

"Well... you just did your first show."

I faked surprise. "What?" I looked around, acting like I was looking for the camera, even though it was in plain sight on the rack of electronic equipment. "You were filming us?"

"Yeah. Please don't be mad! I thought it would be a good way to introduce you to a big group of our fans. You know, get them talking and generate some buzz." She clicked a few buttons on the remote she had, and the chat screen popped up on the big TV.

I saw Reesie on the couch and me lying next to her. I sat up and covered my tits with an arm, and closed my legs. "Holy shit, Reesie! Why didn't you tell me?"

She smiled. "I wanted your first time on cam with us to be authentic and unscripted. I wanted our viewers to see that side of you."

I suppressed a smile. It was anything but unscripted and authentic. Well, the scenario, anyway. The way my body responded to Reesie's touch was utterly genuine. I squinted at the screen. "Are there really eleven thousand people watching us right now?"

Reesie nodded. "Yep! Almost one thousand registered viewers. Hi, guys! What did you think of Ruby?"

She grabbed me and kissed me, full on the mouth. She caught me by surprise, and my hand dropped from my breasts, letting them bounce free. The messages in the chat window next to the video feed were scrolling past almost as fast as I could read them. I broke free from Reesie's mouth and tried to keep up for a few moments, totally forgetting that I was naked. Reesie peppered my shoulder with more kisses while I read the chat.

OctopiWallstreet: I almost lost it just over that red hair. The rest of her is a bonus!

Samwise: I've seen some hot stuff on this site but DAMN

Zaiku: No way this is her first time. No way

DiggDirkler: The red hair Octo? I lost it over the two hotties fucking.

Gollum'sLoinCoth: Anyone see my precious?

OctopiWallstreet: I said almost over the hair. The squirting orgasm put me over the top. I want a closeup of that pussy spread wide!

Luna's handle, in red, indicating she was moderating the chat, popped up.

XXLuna: Easy boys. Don't make me mute you. Save it for the tip chats.

Eddie_69: Shut the fuck up Gollum. Why do you do that shit?

Zaiku: Tip chats haven't been monitored, Luna.

Gollum'sLoinCloth: Gollum.

Reesie stopped kissing me and addressed the camera. "Sorry about that, Zaiku! I sort of had my hands full."

IROC-Z: We heard Ruby moan and cry out in passion... can we hear her say hello?
Zaiku: No worries Reesie, I was just telling Luna.
XXLuna: Luna knows.

I was having a hard time keeping up with everyone, but I caught the request from the person named IROC-Z. I cleared my throat a little. "Hi, IROC. Thank you for watching. I hope you enjoyed it as much as I did." I looked at Reesie. "Reesie is pretty amazing."

DiggDirkler: You're gorgeous Ruby. When will your channel be live? I want to follow you.
Eddie_69: I love your blue eyes.
Gollum'sLoinCloth: My precious.

"I don't know, Digg. I guess I'm not official yet. Thank you, Eddie. Am I your precious, Gollum?"

Reesie jumped in. "Hi, guys! We need more people to sign up for our membership package and vote before Ruby will officially be an XX Camgirl. So, if you're not a member, go hit the link in my bio and sign up!" She reached over and started playing with my nipples, acting like it was something she wasn't even thinking about. "And while we're talking business, for all of you non-registered viewers who want to create an account, wait until Ruby's bio is set up and use her link. She'll get to keep more of your tokens if you use her referral."

Gollum'sLoinCloth: YES! You're my precious! Finally, someone asks me the right question.

A system message, followed by something that sounded like a slot machine paying out, appeared on the screen.

GOLLUM'SLOINCLOTH   TIPPED 1000 TOKENS

The tip chat message, only visible to Reesie and me, read:

*I LOVED WATCHING YOU CUM.
YOU'RE SO HOT! I WISH IT WAS MY
FACE BETWEEN YOUR LEGS.*

Luna had told me the tip notes could get pretty raunchy. I laughed a little at the comment. "Oh, Gollum, that's sweet. I bet you're good at it."

Eddie_69: Oh god, Ruby, whatever he said, don't encourage him.
XXLuna: be nice.
Gollum'sLoinCloth: Eddie's jealous.

Reesie steered the conversation in a different direction. "Ruby, have you ever used the Lovense Lush?"

"No. What's that?"

She flashed a wicked grin. "You're going to love it." She pulled up a box with what looked like a fist-sized pink sperm in it. "This is a Bluetooth-enabled vibrator that our viewers can control with their tips. It has all sorts of settings, and different tip amounts do different things to you. I was thinking we set up a ticket show, and you can use it for the first time tonight. Whaddaya say?"

OctopiWallStreet: Dear lord, say yes!

In for a penny, in for a pound. Besides, it sounded interesting. Though I had a vibrator at home, I didn't use it all that often. I typically didn't need much help getting to an orgasm, and I'm more of a hands-on type of girl. But, under these circumstances, I was obligated to go for it. "I'd love to try it out!"

Reesie beamed. "Great! Luna, can you set a timer for twenty minutes? Ticket prices are two hundred fifty tokens. After ten minutes, the price goes to four hundred, so get in early! VIPs get in for one-hundred for this, and every one of my ticket shows."

A timer started in the chat window. I was so focused on the chat that I forgot I was still naked. I caught a glimpse of my tits bouncing as I shifted positions. I leaned close to Reesie and whispered in her ear. "Can I put on my bra and panties again while we wait on this show? And, I need to pee."

She nodded toward the door to the left of all the equipment. "Yeah, it's through there."

I looked directly at the camera. "Be right back, everyone! I need to... take care of some business." I grabbed my undergarments and scurried into the restroom. I peed for what seemed like forever and put my underthings back on. There was a sign above the toilet that read *Do Not Flush While Camming In Progress!*

I checked my makeup in the mirror. Since I didn't wear a lot, there wasn't much to mess up. My dark eye shadow was smudged a little, and my lipstick was wearing off, but my face wasn't a wreck. My hair, on the other hand, looked like I'd just been fucked within an inch of my life. I messed with it for a minute to make it presentable and went back out to join Reesie.

Eighteen

Tawney lay diagonally across the bed, her torso damp with sweat, out of breath. Gemma returned from the bathroom, naked, and gazed down at the South American vixen. Her many tattoos gave her a mysterious aura, dangerous even, but her spread eagle position made her appear vulnerable. She smiled at Gemma. "I think I'm paralyzed now."

Gemma climbed the bed and scooted between Tawney's long brown legs, running her fingers up the thighs to the wet honey pot that resided where they met. "I can go for another round," she said, teasing the other woman's labia and clitoris, lightly tugging on the patch of black pubic hair.

"Are you trying to kill me? You've become a pussy master since you were here last. Oh, shit, woman. I don't think anyone's ever fucked me that hard."

Gemma glanced up at the TV, then back at Tawney.

"Oh, that's it! You got all worked up watching your girlfriend get devoured by Reesie, and you took it out on me! Oh, now that all makes sense!"

Onscreen, Darcy was sitting on the couch next to Reesie, reading and responding to chat messages while the timer for the ticket show counted down.

"That was hot as hell, wasn't it?" Gemma asked. "I've seen her on video before getting fucked by other people, but this is the first time I've seen her with someone else since we started dating. It was weird, but still a huge turn-on."

"She's good at this, Gemma. A few days, with the girls promoting her, and she could have a popular show. She just needs her gimmick."

"Hopefully, in a few days, we'll have this figured out, and you won't need us here."

Tawney pressed the issue. "Still, she could make some good side income. I'm just saying—"

A knock at the door interrupted her. "It's Luna."

Tawney made no move to cover herself as she went to unlock the door, so neither did Gemma as she laid on the bed.

The door slid open wide enough for Luna to enter the room. She smiled at the scene displayed in front of her. "I see you're conducting a very thorough investigation, Gemma."

"I'm looking in every crevice and hidey-hole I can find."

Tawney fake-laughed. "Haha, Gemma, your turn is coming. I'll be all up in *your* hidey-hole. What's up, Luna?"

"We got the subscriptions."

"Already?"

"Yep. Six hundred twenty-three new subscribers before the ticket show. I just wanted to let you know. I asked Freya to get started on the paperwork, the account, the bio, all that stuff. We should have Ruby up and running tomorrow morning, pending verification."

Tawney smiled. "Perfect! Nice job, Luna."

"Thanks, I need to go start this ticket show." She eyed them both, lingering on Gemma for a few seconds. "As you were, you two. Enjoy the show."

Luna slid the door shut behind her, and Tawney locked it.

"Your girl already brought us sixty-two hundred bucks, Gemma, and she's not even a verified model yet. You sure you want to leave when you figure this thing out?"

"We both have our own businesses to run, Tawney. I don't see how it would work."

"Run them from out here. You both work virtually, so you could do it from here. We can make room for you."

"We own our houses, and mine is going through a major remodel. I'm glad you want us to stay, but we can't."

Tawney sat up and pushed Gemma down on a pile of pillows. She started kissing her on the neck and shoulder. "We'll see. I'll wear you down. If one of you caves, the other will follow."

"Mmmm... Just play with my body while I watch my girlfriend let an audience of ten thousand people control her orgasm."

"Por supuesto, Bellisima."

Nineteen

I looked at the pink sperm. Reesie had kept the chatter going over the last twenty minutes, but now it was showtime. Between VIP club members and people who bought tickets with their tokens, there were over four hundred people in this exclusive portion of the broadcast. All of them were going to watch me insert this device into my vagina, then they were going to spend their tokens to control it. To control me. "Okay, Reesie, so this is called the Lush?"

"Yep. And that one is yours, brand new. I set it up and charged it, but you're taking it out for its maiden voyage! So... strip!"

I gulped. There was no turning back now. I stood and tugged at the waistband of my panties, resisting the urge to just whip them off. I gyrated my hips a bit and lowered them a couple of inches. On-screen, the comments flowed nearly continuously.

Samwise: I love it when women dance like that while getting naked

DiggDirkler: My ex used to strip so I got that all the time. F'n sexy!

OctopiWallstreet: Get ready, Ruby. This is going to blow your mind!

"I hope so, Octo. You guys have built it up so much; I hope it lives up to the hype."

I turned my back to them, showing them my ass as I lowered my panties. I got them down to mid-thigh and stopped. I spun around and covered my pussy with a hand.

Eddie_69: Why so bashful? We've already seen everything.
Zaiku: Chill out, Eddie.
Gollum'sLoinCloth: Gollum.
Eddie_69: GODDAMN IT GOLLUM!

While I was interacting with the chat, Reesie was putting lube on the large bulb of the Lush. "Okay, Ruby. You ready?"

"Yeah, I'm ready. I'm a little nervous!"

"Don't worry, you'll do fine. Right gang? You'll make sure she's taken care of?"

DiggDirkler: Oh, absolutely.
OctopiWallstreet: Yeah, Ruby, you're in good hands.

I sat on the couch and pushed my underwear down past my knees so I could open my legs for Reesie. She smiled at me as she reached for my labia. "I feel like a gynecologist. Just try to relax."

I giggled, unable to suppress it.

> *Zaiku: I didn't enjoy it the last time I heard that.*
>
> *DiggDirkler: I did. My doctor's a woman. I almost nutted.*
>
> *xxLuna: That explains a lot about you Digg.*

Reesie parted my lips, smearing some of the lube on them as she inserted her fingers into me. I let out a moan and lifted my hips. The 'cha-ching' of a tip sounded off. I glanced at the screen. It was from DiggDirkler, and he sent a private tip message.

> *DIGGDIRKLER: FUCK, I LOVE YOU RAISED YOUR HIPS AT REESIE'S FINGERS. YOU'RE FUCKING READY FOR THIS, AREN'T YOU?*

"Yes, I am, Digg. Are you?"

Another tip from Digg with a private message.

DIGGDIRKLER: GODDAMN RIGHT I AM. PANTS OFF, COCK IN HAND. HARD AS STEEL. I'M GOING TO CUM WHEN YOU DO.

"Mmmm... that sounds nice, Digg. I hope you do."

Reesie smiled at me while she increased the pace of her fingers going in and out of me. "You're a natural at this, you know it? You're going to have your fans cumming like mad when you get your own show."

"I hope so. It's kind of hot imagining all these people touching themselves while I have my orgasm."

"Ready for the Lush?"

I pulled my legs up, bending my knees and opening my legs wider. "Please, doctor, put it inside me."

OctopiWallstreet: Here we go!

Reesie pushed the tip of the bulb against my labia, sliding it up and down, pushing them apart. More pressure and I felt the inch and a half of girth pushing inside me, and then it was gone, completely swallowed by my pussy, the five-inch tail the only evidence that it existed at all.

I could feel it inside me. It was an interesting sensation having something that size in me. It felt different from having a cock in me because only the thin bit was sticking out, so my lips were almost fully closed. Reesie turned it on and did her thing with the software to activate the controls for the vibrator. She smiled at me. "Okay, go to town gang. She's all yours."

The tips started moving up the screen. Five tokens, five tokens, five tokens, over and over until the chat window was filled with them. A bunch of names I didn't recognize were in the mix, along with the crew that had been the most active. According to the tip menu, five tokens—about forty cents to the client, about twenty-five cents to XX Cam after the cam company took their cut—bought one second of low vibrations from the device inside me.

There was a slight delay between the tips scrolling by and the Lush activating.

Suddenly, I felt something like a cattle prod electrocuting the inside of my vagina! My hips bucked involuntarily, and I cried out, "Holy fuck!"

The initial shock wore off, but that thing was still vibrating my pussy from the inside. The shape of the bulb had its apex against my G-spot, and the vibrations made me feel like I was going to squirt. All I could do was pump my hips and moan. "Oh my god, oh fuck!"

I heard a different tip tone, and I forced my eyes open to look at the screen. It was one hundred tokens from Octopi.

> *OCTOPIWALLSTREET: GET READY, RUBY. THIS WILL BLOW YOUR SHIT UP!*

I didn't care for my pussy being called *my shit,* but the tip menu said one hundred tokens bought five seconds at high vibration. The device was still processing the five-token tips, and after a few more seconds, the high setting kicked in.

I felt it all the way to my toes. I raised a leg and slid it out of my panties, letting them fall to the floor, my other foot still in the other leg-hole. With no underwear restricting me, I threw my legs wide open and looked down. I felt a little ridiculous with the tail of the Lush protruding from me like a thin pink dick, but whatever, this thing was fucking amazing. My hand launched itself at my clit, and I began rubbing it. "Oh, yeah, fuck," I said, then remembered who brought me this burst of pleasure. "Oh, thank you, Octo."

The vibrations stopped after five seconds. My pussy was still tingling, my pulse pounding in my clit. I let out a big sigh to catch my breath. That was only thirty seconds with this thing. As more tips started pouring in, my mind connected with the fact that I was not in control of this situation. I was at the mercy of a bunch of horny people, men and women, according to Luna, who were virtually manipulating my pussy from around the globe. More, larger tips started coming in. One-twenty-five from Digg, for three seconds of pulse—a sudden jump from low power vibrations to medium, back to low, and back to medium, completing a couple cycles in the three seconds. I responded to as many of the tip comments as I could. Next was five seconds of Wave, an oscillating rise and fall, not a sudden jump and drop like Pulse. "Oh, fuck, you guys, it's like all your hands are in my pussy. It's a virtual orgy!"

A five hundred token tip from Zaiku gave me thirty seconds of *fireworks*—a setting that ratcheted from low to medium to high, dropped to low, and repeated. My head rolled back, and all I could get out were moans and feral sounds. I could understand why this was named fireworks because I was seeing stars. I realized I was grabbing onto Reesie with my right hand and going to town on my pussy with my left. I was so close to cumming, and then the vibrations dropped back down to low.

It was funny; the low vibrations shocked me so much when the tips first started coming in, and now that setting was providing a respite for me. I caught my breath. "Thank you, Zaiku. Holy shit, you felt good."

Zaiku: I do my best.
OctopiWallstreet: You are so hot when you're about to cum.

"Thank you, Octo. You all have me right on the edge. You're torturing me."

The tips kept coming. Five tokens, twenty-five tokens, fifty, one hundred. Every time I was ready to cum, the vibrations would return to low or turn off completely for a second or two, bringing me back from the brink.

The *cha-ching* sound, accompanied by a scream, signaled another one thousand token tip, again from Gollum'sLoinCloth with a private message.

GOLLUM'SLOINCLOTH: WE'VE TEASED YOU ENOUGH. LET ME MAKE YOU CUM.

"Oh, Gollum, what have you done? Thank you!"

Sixty seconds of *Earthquake* began. The Lush stair-stepped up a little from the low setting to something between low and medium, then medium,

152

then between medium and high, then high. There were still at least thirty seconds left on this one.

Another screaming *cha-ching* sounded off. One thousand from DiggDirkler.

The high vibrations continued, then dropped slightly lower and back up to the max several times in quick succession. I was pushed to the edge. "Oh, Gollum, Digg, fuck, you two are going to make me cum!"

And I did. My stomach flexed, and I made some sort of animal noise as my pelvic muscles contracted over and over. My hand was a blur over my clit. "Fuuuuuuuuuck!"

The vibrations dropped off as the Lush processed Digg's tip. The power ramped back up to high, and the quake started again. Oh, my god, I loved this setting. I came again, fluid gushing out of me. The Lush was expelled, and I squirted, as I'm prone to do when my G-spot gets overly stimulated. I grunted, shooting more cum from my pussy. I grunted again, still spasming, but the juices returned to a dribble.

I collapsed, my body a wet noodle on the couch. One leg was still draped over Reesie's lap, my other foot on the floor, my body angled toward the camera. Somewhere, off in the distance, I heard tips being given, but I could not focus. I dragged my hand from my pussy to my tits, using my trimmed fingernails to tickle my skin as they passed over it. I squeezed each of my breasts, pulling on the hard nipples, drawing circles around them. My scalp was tingling, and my toes were numb. Finally, I regained some composure and opened my eyes. My voice was weak when I spoke. "Thank you, Gollum and Digg, for making me come for so long. Holy shit, I'm still caught in the afterglow. Oh my god, that was amazing. All of you are so generous."

I sat up and closed my legs. Feeling how engorged my labia were only reminded me how turned on I was. I just opened my pussy to hundreds of people and let them make me cum. I felt a slight flush return to my cheeks. I absently played with my breasts while I read some of the chat messages.

OctopiWallstreet: Well, I need to get a second job to afford tokens for yet another XXCam girl.

There was a private moderator message from Luna.

XXLUNA: GIRL, I'M SOAKED OUT HERE. YOU'RE IN. YOU'RE SO IN.

I chuckled. "Thanks, Luna! That makes me happy! Can I tell everyone? And Octo, don't go into debt for this. Just tip what you can afford, okay?" Maybe it was just the euphoria of an intense orgasm, but I really did feel grateful to all the people watching, whether they tipped or not. "That goes for all of you. Please don't spend more here than you can afford."

XXLuna: YES, TELL THEM YOU'RE OFFICIAL. 716 NEW MEMBERS.

I looked over at Reesie, and she smiled a wide, toothy grin. "I knew they would love you, Ruby. I knew when we were playing with each other in the pool that you would be a hit."

"You guys," I looked at the screen, not directly at the camera. "You did it! I'm official! I'm going to have my own show!"

Eddie_69: That's awesome Ruby! I can't wait to watch you more! But there's a problem.

I frowned. "What problem?"

DiggDirkler: He's gone blind from beating it!

GurlPerv: You're one to talk.

OctopiWallstreet: GURL! You're back!

GurlPerv: Yeah, haha. Saw Reesie was online and was going to rub one out to her but found this gorgeous redhead instead. I'm soaked.

Eddie_69: The problem is, this is Reesie's room, and she hasn't cum yet.

I smiled at Reesie. "Thank you, Gurl. I'm glad I could do that for you. I'm pretty soaked myself. Now, Reesie, what are we going to do about this problem of Eddie's?"

She turned her body toward me. "Well, I normally have a flow to my shows, but I'm so fucking horny right now. I just want you to eat me until I cum."

I grinned. "What do you say, gang? Eddie, would that solve your dilemma? Let's vote. Five tokens for no, leave Reesie wanting. Ten tokens for yes, Ruby, get in there and make Reesie cum in your face. I'll give you a minute to vote."

I crawled onto Reesie's lap and caressed her face. Behind me, the sound of tips dinging away poured out of the speaker. I ran my hands down Reesie's torso, caressing her breasts and teasing her nipples to hard points. I leaned in and kissed her, my tongue running wild in her mouth.

I pulled away, and Reesie sighed. I stole a glance at the screen. Every tip from top to bottom was a ten-token tip, with multiples from Eddie_69. "Look, Reesie, Eddie's stuffing your ballot box. I guess the ayes have it!"

Twenty

I ravished Reesie for about fifteen minutes until she came in my face. She wasn't a squirter, at least not this time, but her cum was creamy and musky. I loved making women cum, and she was no exception. She caught her breath, and I sat back on the couch in my bra and panties, reveling in the wet face that I was projecting on camera and in the comments of the people watching. They were raving about the performance we'd just given them. Reesie and I sat and chatted with the viewers for another twenty minutes. Even though we weren't doing anything sexual, the tips continued to come in, including another thousand token tip from Gollum.

I was still feeling horny, so we offered a second ticket show, and I had Reesie put the Lush inside me again. This time she wrapped the pink tail upwards, so the vibrating nub at the tip was touching my clit. I was getting the vibrations inside against my G-spot and outside on my button, which took the sensation to a higher level than before. The tips racked up while wave after wave of pleasure rolled through me. I came again but cried out for them to keep going. I don't know how long I came or how many times. I think I was rolling along from orgasm to orgasm for ten minutes. The viewers would tip repeated five token tips to get the one second low vibrations going, edging me for a minute or two, then someone would give in and tip one of the higher amounts to give me the more intense vibes for a longer duration, and it would push me off the edge into another orgasm. At some point, I finally collapsed on the couch, gasping for air, my torso sweaty, my stomach and pelvic muscles spent from contracting. "No more!" I heard myself say in a weak voice. "I can't take any more."

Reesie had been doing all the chatting with the group once I entered the throes of pleasure. She lovingly stroked my legs, and I felt her hand on me as she extracted the Lush. My pussy felt empty but was still tingling from the persistent vibrations. I closed my eyes, the sounds of the chat and Reesie's responses far away. Every now and then, her hand would rub my belly or stroke my calf—some sweet gesture to let me know she was there for me. I ran my hands over my breasts and my stomach, absently tickling myself with my fingernails. I was completely sated.

Gradually, I recovered my senses. I sat up and smiled.

Eddie_69: It is alive!!
Lustinme: She's so blissed out!

"Hi, Eddie. Yeah, I'm alive. Oh my god, you guys have no idea what that was like. I may never be the same."

DiggDirkler: Save some for YOUR shows, Ruby!

It took me a second to remember my stage name was Ruby. The Lush had almost vibrated my memory away! "I will, Digg."

I reached down and found my underwear and slid them up and over my hips.

"Hey guys, I don't know about you, but that was one of the hottest things I have ever witnessed! Ruby really stole the show tonight!" Reesie leaned over and kissed me, her tongue swirling around mine for a few seconds. My stomach did a flip, and I realized, sated or not, I would let her fuck me again if she wanted to. Jesus, I was *all in* on this. I was *loving* it! She broke off the kiss and continued. "Thank you for making me cum, Ruby. I came again while you were getting vibed half to death. You're going to crush it in this business." She turned to the camera. "Right, guys? If you came tonight while Ruby gave her all for you, tip five tokens now and pay your respects! Come on, even you lurkers that never tip, she laid it all out there for you guys! You can pay tribute at least once!"

The five token tips started rolling up the screen and didn't stop for fifteen seconds. I lost track, but it was dozens of them. Knowing that so many people had masturbated to me, and the mental image it conjured in my head, was both a little disturbing and thrilling at the same time. On the one hand, society frowns upon people who masturbate to online porn, but on the other hand, that was the whole purpose of this site. And Reesie and I were not just anonymous faces in video clips; we were live women talking directly to these people, taking their money in trade for a performance. They were *involved* with us, directing us. They'd just used technology and teamwork to virtually fuck me until I came, and I begged them for more, more, and more. It made sense that, on their side, they'd have had one hand on the keyboard and the other in their pants. They gave me several orgasms; it was only right they should get some for themselves. I felt myself flush, heat rising in my cheeks as I watched the tips scrolling by. "Aw, you guys, no way! You all came while watching me? That's amazing! I'm so glad you all got off too."

We chatted with the group for another ten minutes before wrapping up for the night. Once the feed turned off, Reesie clicked through her broadcaster's interface. She gasped and turned to me. "Holy shit, Ruby. We brought in more than *fifty thousand* tokens tonight! That's almost double my record!"

I was incapable of doing the math in my head. "What's that mean to us?"

"Between that and the membership sales, we pulled in about ten grand tonight. Most of that from the memberships."

I was stunned. In my consultancy, I averaged around fifty-two hundred a month. We doubled that in one night. Once again, I thought back to Gemma's warning about getting enamored with this life, and it made even more sense now. I could totally see how it could happen.

I checked the time. We'd been on-air for about five hours. That meant we made two thousand an hour. It was an insane amount of money. I voiced that opinion. "That seems like an unrealistic amount of money."

"Well, tonight was a special deal, and it's right after a payday, so people have money to spend."

"What's a typical night for you?"

"Depends. On average, I'd say I pull in about eight hundred from shows, three nights a week, plus another couple hundred a week from merchandise and videos."

"So you're pulling in about twenty-six hundred a week."

"Yeah, give or take. It sounds like a lot, but California is expensive to live in. If we didn't have a dozen of us shacked up in this house, I don't know if it would be enough."

"Plus, your money is all sent to the main account, right? Luna was explaining that to me earlier."

"Yeah. Tawney and Gemma worked it out a while back that tax-wise, it would be better to pool it all as an LLC. Tawney takes out money for the mortgage on this place, utilities, the website upkeep and maintenance, Maya and Freya's time, all that crap, and it's all tax-deductible, then she pays us out of whatever's left. It works out pretty well, to be honest, but I don't know all the details. I probably should, but it's just one less thing for me to worry about, you know? I have enough to do what I want with."

I thought about my consultancy and the way I leveraged the tax code to reduce my operating income. I struggled with the process every year, and my expenses and revenue sources were pretty basic. I couldn't imagine the kind of overhead they were working with here. "Does everyone make about the same?"

"Oh, no. Luna makes more than most. She's probably in the five thousand per week range. Ginger and April are the other new girls; they're probably in the fifteen hundred to two thousand range. You won't see two grand a week, just FYI. Not for a while, at least. You'll get some bleed-over viewers from tonight, but you'll take a while to build your core audience. But every bit you bring in helps! I'm excited to have you because we're down to eight cam girls with Mercedes leaving. It's worrisome when people leave, and no one replaces them."

I felt a pang of guilt. I knew I wouldn't be here long term, so I was building up people's hopes that I knew I would dash in a week or so once we got the money theft sorted out. That reminded me, I needed intel. "So, we touched on this by the pool earlier...but I need to know, is this money theft thing going to be a serious problem? Do I need to be worried about it?"

Reesie hesitated. She only knew me for about eight hours longer than she had earlier, but she decided to trust me with more information. "Okay, here's what I know. The short answer is yes, it's a huge problem for us. We pull in, combined, about eighty thousand a month. Tawney keeps a percentage of our money in reserve, so we have a safety net, you know, in case there's a recession or something? We can weather the storm. Well, we lost about five full months of revenue. So, we're basically operating month to month right now. The longer answer is Alexis—or Gemma... I don't think she's using her stage name anymore—is back to help figure out who has been taking the money, so hopefully, we can get at least some of it back and stop anyone from getting into it in the future."

"Do you have any thoughts about who's been taking it?"

"Not really." Her eyes narrowed. "Remember, if any of the girls tell you that Tawney is behind it, you don't listen to them. The one thing I know for certain after all these years working with Tawney is that you can trust her. If you have questions, you ask Luna or me, and if we're not around, you ask Tawney. Along with Gemma, the four of us built this business. We're not going to let it fail."

I nodded. Other than Maya, no one had suggested to me that Tawney was behind the money theft, but that must be one theory going around, or Reesie wouldn't warn me off it repeatedly. "So, you don't think any of the newer girls are behind it?"

She paused again. "I don't think so. She wasn't new, but I'm still suspicious of Mercedes. She left for that strip club so soon after it all started... the timing is suspicious. But it's almost too convenient to blame her, you know? Like, if this were an episode of *Midsomer Murders,* she'd be the prime suspect who really didn't do it."

"The red herring," I said.

"Yeah, I guess. But this is life, right? Not a TV mystery."

"Yeah. Occam's Razor usually applies."

Reesie looked at me blankly.

"The simplest explanation is usually the right one. It's called Occam's Razor."

She tilted her head a little. "What made you want to get into this business, anyway, Ruby? You're what, late twenties? Obviously, you have a head on your shoulders and a vocabulary to match. I would think you'd have your life sorted out by now. Most new girls are ten years younger than you."

I'd made her suspicious, but I was ready for this line of questioning. I'd prepared a back story for this, based in part on recent events in my life. "Well, I have a work-at-home job, but it doesn't pay as much as I would like, so I wanted to find something as a side gig. I tried driving for Uber, but it just wasn't enough. It was too much time investment for too little return, you know? I really wanted something else I could do from home. Then I had an affair with a married couple—"

"A couple? As in you were sleeping with them both?"

"Yes."

"At the same time? Like a throuple?"

"No, not like that. Neither one knew I was fucking the other one, which is what made it an affair. Or, I guess, *two* affairs? Anyway, of course, they eventually found out about it, and it ended very badly. They made a revenge porn video of me and posted it on a porn site. It got a lot of views, which bothered me at first, but then I saw a sidebar ad for camming. I thought, 'if people are watching me online anyway, I might as well get paid for it.' So, I did some research, and this seemed like a good thing to try. And I found articles about XX Cam, the all-female cam company, and I decided *fuck it,* and I put my stuff in storage, sold my car, and headed here."

"Why'd you fuck both of them? I've never known anyone who's done that."

She was fixated on the affair, but that was good. Since it was the truth, I could speak to it and not have to remember any lies. "It wasn't like I had some master plan or anything. I went to college with the husband, and we bumped into each other one day. One thing led to another, and—"

"And his dick was inside you."

I smiled. "Yeah, that pretty much sums it up. This went on for a few weeks, and then one weekend, I bumped into him and his wife at the store. I wanted her the second I saw her. It was like

I didn't really have a choice. A fire was lit inside me, and I was hitting on her before I knew it. Turned out she was into it. So, I was suddenly up to my tits in dick and pussy."

"When it rains, it pours."

"I suppose that's true. Anyway, once I got over the shock of seeing myself getting fucked online, this wasn't such a big leap for me."

My story satisfied her curiosity. "Well, I'm glad you're here. And you did great tonight, Ruby. You really did. Now, you should get some sleep. We work out in the morning at eight. It's not mandatory, but I do recommend it. Staying in shape really helps with your on-camera presence. Then you'll go out and do a few remotes in the afternoon. You'll probably go with Amber since you're rooming with her. It will give you two a chance to get better acquainted."

I started gathering all my clothes.

"Oh, Ruby?"

"Yeah?"

"Leave the bra and panties. We have the auction going on them, remember?"

"Oh, yeah. I love this set. Too bad."

"Don't worry, you can buy a dozen of them with the money you'll get from them."

I slid the panties off, handed them to her along with the bra, and walked naked to my room, where my roommate was already in bed, lightly snoring. I suddenly felt like I was a freshman in college again.

The events of the day caught up with me as I crossed the room, and I was suddenly exhausted. I dropped my clothes and the box containing the Lush on the foot of the bed, peeled back the covers, and slid between the sheets. I rolled onto my side, contemplating my new identity as Ruby, the cam girl. I liked everyone I'd met so far, and I *loved* the sex I was having. I felt a pang of guilt, knowing that Gemma was probably watching me tonight. Was I being overly sexual to sell my cover story? Or was I using this opportunity to get as much sex as I could outside of my normally monogamous relationship? Was I being unfair to Gemma? We had texted earlier and discussed her sleeping with Tawney. I wasn't too keen on it, but I couldn't be upset if she did, given what I was doing. And it's not like Tawney is someone you could tune out. I gave her my blessing, but part of me hoped she wouldn't do it, while the rest of me would feel better if she did. These troubling thoughts simmered for a few moments before I drifted off to sleep.

Twenty-One

"You were fucking amazing last night, Ruby." Tawney gave me a long hug. "Are you okay today? No regrets? You don't have to keep this up if you don't want to."

I looked at Gemma, remembering my internal conflict as I drifted to sleep the night before. "I feel like I'm not being fair to you. It's like I have a hall pass or something. I feel like I'm overdoing it and rubbing it in your face, and I don't want this to cause problems for us." I was shocked that my voice quivered, and I was suddenly close to crying.

Gemma pulled me into her arms. "Oh, Darcy, don't worry about that! I know you're playing a role. So am I. We both came into this with our eyes open. I've lived this life! Of course I knew there would be sex involved."

Was she playing a role too? I looked back and forth between her and Tawney. "Did you fuck each other last night?"

Gemma smiled her disarming grin that always melted my resistance to whatever she was going to say next. "Of course we did. We talked about this, Darcy. And do you really think I could watch your performance and *not* have sex?"

I felt a pang of jealousy again, but honestly, it made me feel better. We were both having our fun and obviously still thinking of and focusing on the other.

"Look, Darcy, if it bothers you, Tawney will keep her hands off me for the rest of the investigation. And I will keep mine off her. You're my life now, and I don't want to go back home and have any issues because of this."

"You aren't going to have any issues because of what I'm doing?"

"Not at all. I know you love me. It took *ten years* for us to find each other again. Ten days in California isn't going to undo that. It's just sex, Darce."

"But what if I really like this? I mean, my orgasms were real, Gemma. I'm sorry I'm making a big deal out of this. In the heat of passion, I had zero reservations about what I was doing. But in the light of day, when I'm not horny and orgasmic, I can't help but think that I've betrayed you somehow."

"Do you love me, Darcy?"

"Of course I do! Why would you ask that?"

"Because love is more than sex, Darce. You only betray me if you're not honest with me. I've been where you are. I warned you about getting enamored with this life. Trust me, the allure fades. Just come back to me when this is done, and be honest about everything, and I promise I'll love you more than ever."

"And I'll leave her alone, Darcy. Ruby, I mean."

I looked over at Tawney. For a minute, I'd forgotten this South American goddess was in the room with us. This woman who had simply devoured me less than twenty-four hours ago and twelve hours ago had apparently devoured my girlfriend. With her brazen pink braids and tattoos and caramel skin, her appearance screamed, 'look at me,' but her demeanor said, 'at your own risk.' She projected power and sexuality. As she looked me directly in the eyes, I felt my stomach flip. Jesus, if she told me to strip and get on the bed, I would do it. Even as part of me wanted Gemma to have no further contact with the woman, I wanted her to take me for another ride like yesterday. It was hopeless to resist her. "No, you two have a history. We talked about it. If I get a hall pass, Gemma does too. But when this is over, just remember that she belongs to me."

Gemma giggled. "Gods, I want you so bad when you talk tough. You have no idea how much that turns me on."

Tawney grinned. "I can let you use my room for an hour if you like."

We looked at each other. I was torn. I had stuff to do, but every fiber in my body wanted to rip Gemma's clothes off and take her in front of this wild-haired Amazonian queen.

A knock on the door solved my dilemma.

"Tawney? Is Ruby in there? I'm ready to head out for her remotes."

I grabbed Gemma's hand. "Amber, my roomie. I guess I should go."

She laced her fingers through mine and squeezed, pulling me in for a kiss. "Go, have fun. We need to get to the bank anyway."

I tasted her coconut and pear lip gloss, longing for more but knowing it would have to wait. "I love you, Gemma."

"I love you, too, Darcy," she replied. Then her serious face turned smirky. "And I'm kind of hot for Ruby, too."

I laughed and let go of her hand as I turned to the entry. "Coming, Amber!" I started walking to the big sliding door. Tawney walked with me.

"Ruby, thank you again for all you're doing. I know it's a sacrifice, and when this is over, I promise you, I'll make it all up to you."

"Okay. I'm going to hold you to that."

She smiled as she slid the door to the side, revealing Amber on the other side. "Have fun, girls. Where are you headed?"

Amber grinned and stuck her ample chest out. "I'm taking my newbie roomie to the place every California rookie has to go. Beverly Hills!"

Twenty-Two

Amber was an enthusiastic beauty. Her alarm went off at seven-thirty. I heard her fumble to turn it off, then was startled when she screamed, "Roomie!" She leaped from her bed and ran over to mine, diving on me and squealing with delight. I tried to fend her off, but I was too tired, so I gave up.

She snuggled against me, gave me hugs and kisses, and told me how glad she was to have a new person in her life. I just wiggled and settled against her in the little spoon position, hoping she'd let me get a few more minutes of rest.

"You didn't get mad," she said.

"About what?"

"About me attacking you first thing in the morning, accosting your gorgeous naked body with mine. Most people I've roomed with hated that. Even Mercedes didn't like it. I find if you can deal with that, you'll be able to deal with me the rest of the time."

"I had a dog when I was a kid. He used to greet me like that every morning, jumping on me and licking my face until I got up. Sometimes I hated it and just wanted to be left alone to sleep, but after we had to put him down, I missed it. Every morning I wanted nothing more than for that dog to attack me like that again."

Amber affected a disdainful tone. "Are you comparing me to a dog?"

"No, I—"

"Because I love it! Dogs are the greatest creatures on earth. They approach life with unconditional love. It'd be a better world if we all were more like dogs."

She kept her momentum rolling, telling me that she was originally from Arkansas but said there were only two things that she brought with her; a southern accent which only came out when she was either really excited or really pissed off, and a love for cutoff jean shorts.

Amber's real name was Leslie David, and she was thirty-two years old, making her the oldest woman in the house aside from Tawney and Luna. She said her age was starting to concern her because the cam industry seemed to be moving to younger women and people began to age out around age thirty. "It's like Logan's Run," she said. I didn't get the reference, and her jaw dropped. "You never saw Logan's Run? I have the DVD. We'll have to watch it. You'll totally get the reference then."

"You know how I know you're old?"

She looked at me, her smile fading a bit. "No, how?"

"You still have DVDs."

She shoved my shoulder playfully. "You're sassy! I like that. We're going to be good friends, I can tell. You want to go work out with me?"

I didn't, but I remembered my conversation the night before with Reesie. Besides, it would give me a chance to scope out the other girls.

I watched Amber as she got ready to head to the gym in the basement. She had long dishwater blonde hair that cascaded down her back, stopping about six inches above her ass. Her face was freckled girl-next-door, set with bright blue eyes and full, pouting lips. She was tan all over and had tattoos from shoulder to wrist on each arm, but nowhere else on her body—and she had shown me all of it. She was on the short side, maybe five foot five, with slender arms and a skinny body topped with a long, thin neck. The features that stood out, though, were her huge breasts. I was guessing 34DD, and from the amount of sway and bounce, they were natural.

I got up, dressed in my workout clothes, and went to the basement with Amber for a high-intensity impact training session taught by Diamond. Her real name was Eliza Montoya, and she was another Amazon goddess. Five feet, ten inches tall, one hundred fifty pounds of muscle, and smooth brown skin. She had jet black hair, brown eyes, and no tattoos. She wore a pair of short, tight yoga shorts and a sports bra that held her breasts in check. With her broad shoulders and muscular build, she was probably carrying 38Cs, which would be the equivalent of 36Ds. Her belly was just shy of showing her six-pack, but certain movements highlighted the ridges of muscle. She looked like an action movie star.

After she was through with us, Amber and I returned to our room, where she let me shower first so I could go meet with Tawney. The pretense Tawney used was that she needed to go over a bunch of onboarding stuff with me, and no one raised a manicured eyebrow at the logic, so they must have all gone through something similar.

There really were a few things she had to cover with me, but we mostly talked about what I had learned from the girls thus far, which didn't really amount to much, other than Reesie telling me that some of the girls thought Tawney was behind the theft.

I thought she'd be mad, but she laughed. "Figures. I suspect one of them is behind it, and they think I'm the one doing it. Perfect."

After Amber came and got me, we hopped in her Lexus RC 300 Sport. The two-door coupe was sleek and sexy, black exterior and a black and gray interior, and was new enough that she still had the temporary tags on the back. I slid into the passenger seat while Amber put a bag behind the driver's seat. She settled behind the wheel and started the engine. It purred to life, and *Saint Cecilia* by the Foo Fighters began blasting from the speakers. Amber turned the volume down to a reasonable there's-other-people-in-the-car level, flipped a U-turn, and immediately turned right onto the narrow road that my Uber had ascended yesterday.

Amber drove fast—not dangerously so—and I felt centrifugal force pulling me to one side of the car and then the other as we whipped down Thrasher Avenue to Rising Glen Road, where she turned right.

Amber's foot shot the Lexus to forty miles per hour in just a few seconds, much faster than what my Mini Cooper back home could do. We approached a stop sign, and Amber pointed to a house on the right side of the road. "Bobby Darin and Sandra Dee used to live there. It's a landmark now."

The Lexus pulled away from the stop sign, rounded a corner, and had to stop at the next intersection as well. After that, Amber's foot was on the gas, the car turning hard to the left, then back to the right around a hairpin curve, then back to the left, the right, and the left again. Though the road was narrow, it was wider than Thrasher Avenue, and Amber had a joyous look on her face as she swept from curve to curve. "I paid an extra grand for sport suspension in this thing. It fucking rips through this canyon. I love it!"

I was grateful for the seatbelt. We finally arrived at a bigger intersection. "This is the famous Sunset Boulevard," she explained. She pointed to the left. "Just there is Wahlburgers. You know, the place Marky Mark and his brother opened? They have good food. And if you go that way for a ways, you'll hit Laurel Canyon and Mulholland Drive. I'm sure you've heard of them. We can go put the car through its paces there later if you want."

My stomach was still feeling the effects of the descent down the canyon. "That's okay. Maybe another day."

"Okay, anytime, just let me know. I looove to drive this thing."

Amber was relentlessly cheerful as she navigated through traffic. At the stoplight at Clark Street, she pointed to the building on the corner. "Whiskey a Go-Go," she said, apparently assuming that I would know all about it. The marquee read

Friday Only Six Demon Bag
With Smollet's Folly

I had actually heard of Six Demon Bag before. I liked their cover of New Order's *100 Miles Per Hour*.

A few blocks later, Amber pointed to the right again. "There's the Roxy."

The marquee here read:

> *Fri – Curves From Below w special guest Buttered Toast Sat – Half Day War   Sun – Gun Show Loophole.*"

"Wow, this is a great location. You're super close to so many options for entertainment," I commented.

"Yeah, there's live music every night, all over the place." She pointed over her shoulder, to the left. "Back that way is the Viper Room, you know, where River Phoenix died? There are so many iconic places!"

We stayed on Sunset as it bent to the left, and we passed between two tall buildings. The one on the right had an Italian restaurant taking up a spot on the ground floor. "That place is really good. I saw Jack Nicholson there a year or so ago."

"How was he? Did you get his autograph?"

Amber scoffed. "No. You don't ask for autographs if you live in LA, and you don't go up to someone like him and ask for one in any case."

We kept driving, and a few seconds later, my heart actually skipped a beat. On the right side of the road, planted right next to a crosswalk, was a sign.

BEVERLY HILLS.

Twenty-Three

Amber continued along the narrow four-lane-divided road. The businesses gave way to a residential area, though that was an assumption. It could have been anything on the other side of the tall white fences and solid green mass of hedgerows, and I'd never know the difference. I tried peering into the occasional driveway that cut through the tall hedges, but there was always a gate, and the house was blocked from view.

The grass in the median strip was dead. Amber pointed it out and said, "They quit watering the grass when we were in the middle of the drought. So all over the place, you'll see huge spots where it's just basically dirt for the landscaping."

"I guess that makes sense."

A few blocks later, I caught a good view of a house—a mansion, rather—off to our right. It was a massive two-story affair with four chimneys, a balcony in front of every set of tall windows on the second floor—though I suppose they must have been doors, not windows—and a massive two-story arched entryway. I thought I saw a fountain too, but in a second, we were past it, and the trees again blocked my view.

We continued on Sunset to North Beverly Drive, passing through the million-dollar homes on the street lined with palm trees. We took a right on Santa Monica, then a left on—holy shit!—*the* Rodeo Drive. Jesus, I really was in Beverly Hills, California. Swimming pools, movie stars. Amber turned right on Brighton Way and pulled into a parking garage. Like she drove on the streets, Amber took the turns a little too fast, the car's tires squealing on the smooth concrete of the lanes and ramps. Up, up she went, going in circles until we reached the rooftop. There were only four other cars here on this top deck. She backed into a parking spot.

I looked over at Amber. "Why the top deck?"

She got a devilish grin. "Well, we're here to shoot your remotes. These are videos you'll sell on your bio page in the broadcasting application to get more tokens, and members on our website can download ten per month for free and then pay for extra for any after that. You'll produce more than just those ten, though, so there's always more content than they can download for free."

"Which means they go buy them with tokens?"

"Yeah, you're getting it! Or they can pay cash on the website. Either way, if they like what you're putting out there, it's extra money in your pocket."

"So, we're on the roof because...."

"Your first few shoots are viewer requests. And the first one is to masturbate in public, specifically in the car."

She handed me a sheet of paper with some shot notes, things to keep in mind while filming, and a generic introduction and ending script. She pointed to those sections. "Don't read them word for word, or it will sound too forced. Just hit the high notes. Let me know when you're ready."

While I looked over the instruction sheet, Amber set up a small camera mounted to some sort of holder attached to the air vent on the dash. Then she grabbed a second camera and fussed with it for a minute. She saw me looking at her quizzically. "It's for multiple angles. I'll give these to Freya and Maya, and they'll edit them together and post them on the website."

"Okay, gotcha."

I continued reviewing the notes for a minute and was confident I had what I needed to do. I handed the paper back to Amber. She put it back in the bag and smiled at me. "You ready?"

I gulped. The cam show the night before was one thing. I had Reesie there, and I was already hot for her from our time in the pool, so it was no big deal to get in the mood to have sex with her. Now, it was just me and the camera. "How long do we go for?"

"The video should be around ten minutes. If you need to go longer, that's okay, but don't go too much shorter."

"Okay." I took a deep breath. "Let's do it."

She set both cameras to record and did a movie-esque countdown. "Okay, mark on my voice and start in five, four, three, two..." and she pointed at me when she was on the 'one' count. It was go time.

"Hi everyone! It's me, Ruby, your newest XX Camgirl. We're still getting my schedule set up, but we really wanted to say thank you to the new members who signed up during Reesie's show last night. So, I'm out today with Amber doing some remote shoots for you all to enjoy in the meantime."

Amber spun the handheld camera and smiled at the lens. "Hi, gang! I can promise you, this is going to be hot!"

She flipped it back around to me. "So, Amber told me that you guys all got to vote on what I had to do today. And the first one was to masturbate in public. We're here in Amber's car, and I'm going to take care of business here in this parking lot in Beverly Hills!"

I looked around and saw some sort of sports car pulling into a spot about fifty feet from us, and a couple was walking toward a range rover a few spaces away from there. I pointed, and Amber took the cue to swing the camera and film through the windshield as I continued the narration. "As you can see, this is an active lot, with people coming and going right in front of us." It clicked in my head what I had just said. "Which is good because someone's going to be cumming in here, too."

I let the joke settle for a minute and started running my hands on my breasts and stomach. "Mmm. Let's get this party started, shall we?"

It took a second to get my head around masturbating for the camera. I rubbed one hand over my groin and the other over my breasts. The notes said there was a formula for this kind of video, and the intent was to have the viewer get more and more excited, and ideally, they would cum when I did. To affect that, the whole thing must have escalating risk. It all made sense. I just hoped I could pull it off and make it look natural.

I undid the buttons on my shorts and lifted my hips, and, hooking my thumbs in the waistband of my panties, I slid them down to mid-thigh. I'd always been able to make myself cum with just my fingers, so I was going to start with that. I had the Lush in the console in the event I got stage fright.

I ran my fingers through my soft burgundy pubic hair and started rubbing my clit, feeling that familiar surge of electricity that spread through my body whenever I touched myself. Motion caught my eye, and I saw a car pulling in and parking off to my left. I instinctively pulled my shorts up a little way. "Oh, shit, you guys, someone just pulled in next to us!"

Amber aimed her camera out the window and filmed the guy walking away from his car, right past us. He was engrossed in a call, talking to his Bluetooth headset, and never even looked our way as he headed to the elevator.

I pushed my shorts back down and resumed touching myself. I felt myself get wet, my fingers suddenly soaked with my juices. That further excited me. I wanted to touch my nipples, but my bra was in the way. So, I sat up and reached around my back to unhook the clasp, pulled my arms inside my shirt and through the shoulder straps, then pulled it through my sleeve. My nipples hardened as the lacy fabric slid over them. When I laid back against the seat, they were poking through the shirt.

I resumed touching my pussy, sliding a finger through my slit, loving the sensation of my lips being pushed apart. For the first time in a long time, I felt a desire to have a nice cock open my pussy and fill it up with its girth. I plunged three fingers inside to simulate that feeling while my other hand twisted at my nipples. Without my consent, an "Oh, fuck," escaped my throat.

The fabric of my shirt was bothering me, so I pulled it up, exposing my breasts, and resumed pulling on my nipples. My hips bucked at the skin-on-skin sensation. I tried spreading my legs wider so I could plunge my fingers deeper, but my shorts got in the way. I pulled my left leg up and out of the shorts and panties. I tried to kick them off my right leg, but the fabric folded in on itself, and it wouldn't get clear of my foot. In an act of frustration, I reached down and pulled them off my foot, and threw them in the back seat. I realized right after I did that, should someone come by the car, I was naked from the waist down, and there was nothing I could do to cover up. The thought excited me. I crossed my arms and pulled my shirt over my head, throwing the shirt over the seat too. Now I was completely naked, wet, and ready to start touching myself again.

I ran my fingers from north to south, tickling my clit, splitting my lips apart, and tickling and teasing my asshole. That sent another charge through my body, and I resumed sliding my fingers in and out of my pussy, using my thumb on my clit with every downstroke. I moaned, waves of pleasure forcing air past my vocal cords.

I was getting close to cumming. I didn't know how many minutes had elapsed – was it long enough for a good video? – and thinking about the clock pulled me back from the edge. I was breathing heavy and starting to sweat.

Of course, I was sweating! We were in the sun in a parked car with the engine, and AC turned off so they wouldn't interfere with the audio. "Fuck, it's hot in here." I reached over and pulled the door release, pushing it open a few inches and letting some air in.

"Oh, fresh air, that's better." I put my right foot on the dash and my left on the console between the seats, angling my pussy toward the camera. I had myself back on the edge, but I wasn't quite able to tumble into my orgasm. I was sure by now it had been ten minutes. I debated getting the Lush out, but instead, I pushed the door all the way open. Anyone driving or walking past the car would have a full view inside and see me, completely nude, legs spread, finger fucking myself, and tweaking my nipples. I dipped my pinky into my pussy, and with a bit of contortion, got my hand in position. On the next stroke, I let my pinky drive into my asshole. "Oh, fuck! Oh, fuuuuck!" I pushed in, driving my fingers as deep as they would go. The way they were contorted, they were brushing my g spot, bringing myself to the very edge of my orgasm. As I worked my fingers in and out, I caught movement in my periphery. I turned my head to the right and locked eyes with a man and his wife as they drove past the car. The woman's eyes went wide, and I expected her to get angry, but it looked like she said, "holy shit!" And broke into a huge grin.

My hips convulsed as I began to cum. "Oh, fuuuck, I'm cumming, I'm cumming!" I screamed at the couple. To my surprise, he stopped the car, and the couple just stared at me while I fucked myself with my hand. I kept my eyes on them but spoke to my viewers. "I hope. You can. See this." My breath was coming in gasps as I continued to cum. "They're both. Looking right. At me. Oh, fuck!" Another wave of pleasure as I said out loud that the couple was staring at me. "Fuck, I'm cumming still. She's locked eyes on me. I can't stop cumming. Can't stop. Fucking myself."

The woman sat up straight. I could see she was wearing a thin-strapped tank top. She hooked her thumbs into the straps and pulled them to the sides and down, exposing her breasts to me.

"Oh my god! Her tits! Oh, fuck!" Without warning, I squirted, shooting my juices onto the dashboard where it ran down and dripped onto the floor mat. I shut my eyes and felt my hips bucking, seeking my fingers that continued to slip in and out of my pussy and ass. I finally stopped convulsing and withdrew my drenched hand. When I opened my eyes, the car was gone.

I rolled my head toward the camera, out of breath, my heart pounding and my pussy vibrating of its own accord. "Holy shit, guys. That was fucking intense. See you next time."

I let the camera continue running, assuming that Freya and Maya would edit the footage. I looked around the car, and Amber was gone. I felt a moment of panic until she appeared on my side of the vehicle.

"Ruby...You've got a fan club."

I looked out the open car door and saw a row of fifteen people, mostly, but not all, men, lined up along the windows of the office building behind us. From their vantage point, they could see at least eighty percent of my naked body in the car, meaning they had seen the whole thing. I hung my head in embarrassment, covering my face with my hands.

"They love you, Ruby! Come on, give them a bow!"

The entire group was applauding. *Fuck it.* I swung my leg out and stood up, holding my arms wide and exposing myself to the group, then did my best theatrical bow. They went wild for it. I looked at Amber. "Okay, can we go now?"

She smiled behind the camera. "Yeah, we can go."

Twenty-Four

We visited several stores along Rodeo Drive, trying on clothes and filming each other in the dressing rooms, of course taking off more clothes than was necessary, kissing and fondling each other. We got a lot of good footage for the website, and I picked up a couple new sets of lingerie, including a couple of bra and panty sets to replace the one from the previous night that I would be losing to the auction.

"What's next?"

Amber fussed with her camera, making sure that everything was saved, before answering. "Well, we got a lot of good footage today. We hit the shots I wanted to. Why don't we walk down Rodeo a bit since you've never been here, and then we can go back to the house, hand everything over to Maya and Freya, and fool around a little? You've made me super horny."

A woman turned toward her and gave her a look as she walked past. Amber just laughed. She grabbed my hand and laced her fingers through mine. "Come on."

We walked a couple of blocks south, mostly window shopping then crossed Rodeo and walked back to the north. We reached the crosswalk in front of Battaglia and started across the street. As we passed the huge planters in the median strip, I noticed a black SUV pull from a parking space in front of Gucci. Amber kept walking, saying something about her desire for a Prada handbag overcoming her aversion to the price.

The roar of the SUV's engine drowned out everything else. I looked at it again, frozen for a moment, until it finally registered that it wasn't going to stop. I pushed Amber and screamed at her, "Go! He's not stopping!" She cleared the street a couple of steps ahead of me. I could swear as I got closer to the sidewalk, the front end of the big black beast angled toward me. The passenger tire hopped the curb just past a green Jersey barrier set in place to guard a pair of bistro tables against getting hit by traffic. The back end of the SUV contacted the concrete slab, sending people screaming from the tables.

It was almost on top of me. I leaped as hard as I could, trying to get clear of the big chrome metal mouth of this roaring monster. I felt something hit my foot, and I began tumbling. I saw sky, sidewalk, sky, sidewalk, then hit the ground hard.

My vision went dark. I heard metal crunching, glass breaking, and more people screaming. I heard someone say, "Call the police!"

and another voice cried, "Call an Ambulance." A third voice said, "It's the same number. 911."

I struggled to open my eyes. At first, the light was too bright to handle, but after a few moments, it cleared up, and I saw a familiar face. Amber wore a look of concern, her face clouded with worry, her voice dripping with her southern accent.

"Ruby, are you okay? Holy crap, that was scary!"

The spiderwebs were slowly clearing. I held out my hand, and she helped me sit up. "Yeah, I'm okay, I think." I looked down at my feet. "Where's my shoe?"

Amber looked at my feet. "Oh my god, I didn't even notice!"

"Here is shoe."

I recognized the voice, but it didn't make sense that she would be here. I reached up and took the sandal from the extended hand. My eyes took in the massive diamond on her ring finger and the sleeve of tattoos that started on the back of her hand and ran all the way up to and disappeared inside the black sleeve that hung just off her shoulder. Her black hair, lustrous, spilling over her shoulders, framing the ample cleavage highlighted by the scoop neck. Despite all the drama going on all around me, despite almost being killed by a huge black SUV, my stomach did a flip, and I felt the same sense of attraction as I did when I first met her back at the strip club in Colorado.

"Olenna?"

"Yes, girl. My car is coming. We will take care of you."

A massive wall of a man stood next to her. He spoke into a walkie-talkie in a foreign language while Olenna chatted at him in what sounded like the same tongue. Ukrainian. I remembered she was Ukrainian.

Amber leaned close to me. "Who the fuck is the tattooed rock-n-roll dancer?"

"She's from back home. I met her a week or so ago."

"What does she mean her car is coming?"

"I don't know. Olenna? Olenna?" I tried to get her attention. She finally turned toward me.

"Yes, Darcy?"

"What do you mean 'your car is coming?'"

"It means my car is coming, darling. Just as I say. You rest your head; we will take care of you."

I looked at Amber. "It means her car is on the way."

Amber laughed. "I heard her, Ruby. We should wait for the police and the ambulance."

"I can hear you, too, girl. We will take care of Darcy. No need for ambulance."

Amber stood and got in Olenna's face, seeming much taller than her five foot five inches. "What are you talking about? She's not going anywhere until she's been checked out by an EMT, and I'm not letting her go with you!"

"We have concierge doctor. Better than EMT." Olenna looked Amber up and down. "You will come as well. We all go."

I still couldn't connect Olenna from Poppa Chubby's being here in California. It seemed like an awfully big coincidence that she popped up right after I had a close call with a hit-and-run, and I don't really believe in coincidences. "Olenna, what are you doing here?"

"I am on shopping trip. Poppa's boy has business here in Los Angeles. I made him bring me so I can shop in real stores. Here comes car. Get up."

Amber took my outstretched hand, helping me to my feet. I looked around at the crowd of faces gathered around us. In the distance, I heard a siren, but whether it was the police or the ambulance, I didn't know. Amber tugged at my arm, pulling me close to her, brushing dirt off my ass. "You're not going with her, are you? Who is she?"

I looked back at Olenna. There had to be a reason why she was in California. And with Poppa's boy here, that was even more curious, especially since he was here just before all the money started going missing. There were too many wires crossing here for there not to be a connection to what was happening with XX Cam, and I would never get a better chance to find out what that connection was than with an open invitation to their hotel.

A black SUV pulled up on the opposite side of the street and stopped with the back door over the crosswalk. Olenna strutted toward it. "Come, ladies. We go now."

Amber looked at me with furrowed brows. I didn't want her to freak out. "Text Tawney, tell her what's happened, and that we're going with Olenna. Trust me, we're going to be okay."

I grabbed her hand and hustled after Olenna, leaving the crowd of people behind us muttering and objecting to our exit. We ignored them and slid into the back seat next to Olenna. The black Range Rover launched ahead before the door was even shut. We made a left on Brighton Way, and I saw Amber look wistfully at the parking garage where her Lexus was parked. I patted her leg and nodded to her. I hoped she got the message; everything will be fine.

Olenna leaned forward, looked across me, and nodded toward Amber. "Why does this one call you Ruby?"

Amber leaned forward and looked across me. "Hi! My name's Amber, not 'this one,' just for the record. You are Natasha, and he's Boris, or...?"

"Amber, this is Olenna..." I trailed off. I didn't know Poppa Chubby's last name. Surely, it wasn't really 'Chubby.' Olenna Chubby? No way this beauty would go for that.

"Olenna Tartaryn." The dark-haired beauty extended a hand, and Amber reached across me to shake it. "Pleased. A friend of Darcy is friend of mine."

That seemed to make Amber a little more comfortable. I turned toward her. "Olenna is married to the owner of a strip club back home."

"Poppa Chubby's? The place that Mercedes went to?"

I nodded. "That's the one." I turned to Olenna. "And she's calling me Ruby because that's my screen name. I'm working with Amber at XX Cam. We always use our screen names, so we don't make any mistakes when we're live."

I watched her face to see if she had a reaction to the news. If she was involved with the theft of the money, that revelation would surely raise an eyebrow. Instead, she scanned me from head to foot, looking a little like the Terminator.

"You have good body for camming. You should do well."

The driver made a right on Wilshire while Olenna made a call. She spoke in her native Ukrainian, so I had no idea what was being discussed. She disconnected and immediately dialed another number. "Hello, Junior."

My ears perked up. Poppa's son.

"I hope your meeting was good one. I'm letting you know I'm bringing company back to hotel. Don't be surprised when you find people in room." She pressed end. "I've asked Oleg to get the concierge doctor to room for you, Darcy. And Junior will be bitch if he didn't have a good business meeting. Ignore him if he causes problem. He's not paying for room, Poppa is." She smiled and waved a credit card at us.

"Who's Oleg?" I asked.

"Another Ukrainian. He's loyal to Junior, while Yuri," she gestured at the driver, "is my brother and of course loyal to me."

I had barely noticed Yuri weaving in and out of traffic, but when he made a hard left onto Santa Monica Boulevard, I slid into Olenna, our bodies pressed together against our will for a moment. I smelled her perfume and felt the muscles in her core flex as she resisted the centrifugal force. I whimpered, and Olenna smiled without looking at me.

"Sorry," Yuri said as he straightened the Range Rover and steered to the right, pulling into the entrance for the Waldorf.

Amber craned her neck, looking through the panoramic sunroof at the white edifice of the hotel. She looked at me and winked. "Maybe this was a good idea after all."

Twenty-Five

The suite was massive. When we arrived, Olenna's bodyguard ushered me into a gigantic bedroom where the concierge doctor was waiting for me. Amber sat by my side while Olenna talked with the bodyguard in Ukrainian.

While the doctor examined my foot, Amber showed me her phone. It displayed a message from Tawney.

> *TELL RUBY 'WHATEVER IT TAKES.'*
> *SHE'LL KNOW WHAT THAT MEANS.*

I nodded, and Amber mouthed, "What the fuck?" to me.

"Later," I whispered.

The doctor released my foot and pulled up a chair. "Well, here's the deal, my dear. Your foot is fine. You said it's not sore; I don't see any appreciable swelling that would indicate tissue damage. You'll probably see some bruising, but I think that will be minor.

"Your pupil response is a little delayed. Based on the bump on your head, I believe you've got a mild concussion. How's your pain?"

My hand involuntarily went to the lump on my head. I hadn't noticed it until he found it doing his exam. "It's okay unless I push on it."

He chuckled. "Well, don't do that. I'm going to leave you some hydrocodone. Take one now and then every six hours as needed for the next day. You're at an increased risk for a brain bleed right now, so avoid ibuprofen and aspirin. If you run out of these, take Tylenol. Okay?"

"Okay. And what else? No going to sleep? No activity? What are my limitations?"

"The sleep thing is a myth. Your brain heals while you sleep, so go to sleep on your normal schedule. Take a nap if you need to. No strenuous activity for a few days, okay? Keep an eye out for any cognitive issues, confusion, blackouts—if anything like that happens, get to an ER. Okay? Otherwise, just take it easy for a couple days, and you'll be fine."

"Okay, thanks, Doc."

"My pleasure. Call if you have any questions."

He left me with four packets containing one hydrocodone each. I heard him talk to Olenna outside the door, and a moment later, she walked in.

"Okay, lovelies. Come, we have the spa here to erase the adventure of the day. Come!"

Amber and I exchanged looks. Mine was meant to say "What the fuck" but hers said "Yes!!!"

We followed Olenna to the enormous living room. It was built to host parties, with a wall of large windows looking out over Beverly Hills. A massage table sat near the windows, with a tall, thin Latina woman standing next to it. A manicure station faced one of the chairs, and a pedicure station sat in front of another. Two young, beautiful Asian women beamed at us from their places in front of their equipment.

Olenna gestured toward the impromptu spa. "Go, ladies. Darcy, you get massage first. Amber, you want mani or pedi first?" Olenna still refused to use my screen name.

"Oh, pedi, please, if that's all right."

"Of course!"

Amber squealed and ran to the pedicure station, her initial reluctance to accompany Olenna completely forgotten.

I approached the massage table. The therapist beamed at me with perfectly aligned, brilliantly white teeth. "Hello, you're Darcy, right?"

"Yes."

"I'm Mia. I understand you've had a rough day." She reached out and rubbed my shoulders with soft hands which had a firm grip.

"Yeah, you could say that, Mia. A massage will be nice."

"Good, we'll get you all taken care of. Go ahead and disrobe and climb on the table. I'll start you face down." She grabbed a sheet and held it in front of me like a curtain, shielding me from the view of the others in the room. I was already naked all over the internet, so while it was a nice gesture, it wasn't necessary.

I took my shirt and bra off, shimmied out of my shorts and panties, and slid onto the table. I nestled my face in the cradle while Mia draped the sheet over my naked body.

She started by having me inhale the vapors from peppermint oil. "It will help you relax." It smelled good, and maybe it's just because she told me to, but I did feel my weight settle into the table as the tension left my muscles.

She placed a hand in the center of my back and kept it there while she walked from one side of the table to the other, adjusting the sheet and how it covered me. I liked the feeling of her hand being anchored as a pivot point.

Mia started rubbing my back, running her hand from the top of my ass to the base of my neck. "Let me know if the pressure is okay. I'll start with moderate, but I can go harder or softer."

I resisted the urge to make a harder vs. softer joke. Mia kneaded the muscles on the right side of my back for a few moments. "You can go harder than that. I like it really firm." I heard Amber chuckle. "Yeah, yeah, I know Amber, that's what *she* said."

"Well, you did say it, so it's true."

Mia dug into the muscles up and down the right side of my back. She used that same hand in the middle of my back pivot maneuver to cross to the left side, and she started in, finding a knot in my left shoulder right away. I started to drift off, my consciousness limited to the places on my body Mia's strong hands were manipulating. She covered my back with the sheet and uncovered my legs. I heard her reapplying her massage lotion to her hands, and she started on my hamstrings.

I was drifting again when I felt a second pair of hands on me. I lifted my head to see who it was, but I heard Olenna's voice say, "No, no. Put head down. Relax. Four hands better than two."

Olenna started on my left hamstring while Mia worked on the right one. Her hands were strong, and the pressure was a close match to Mia's. She moved up higher, pressing her thumbs into the crease where my ass cheek met my thigh, applying pressure all the way to the inside of my thigh, stopping just shy of the base of my labia.

I whimpered.

"Yeah? You like?" Olenna repeated the move, this time just contacting my pussy. My body responded to her touch by flooding my opening with slick juice. Before I knew what I was doing, I moved my left leg to the edge of the table, pressing it into Olenna.

"Good girl. Let Olenna help you." I moaned when she said that and again when she slid a finger into my slit. I lifted my hips to afford her better access, and more fingers joined the first. On the right side of my body, Mia kept working on my leg as though nothing was going on.

I gasped when a pair of lips brushed against my neck, and a third pair of hands were on me, fingers twining through my hair. "Amber?"

"Shh. Relax." Amber's voice was liquid in my ear. She pulled my earlobe into her mouth and sucked on it. The sheet slid off me, leaving me naked and exposed. Amber kissed her way across my shoulders, her lips forming a seal, sucking to pull the skin tight, and brushing my skin with her tongue. Sometime while this was happening, Olenna and Mia traded positions, and Mia started working on my left leg while Olenna kept fucking me with her fingers. I felt my hips pumping against her hand, though I wasn't conscious of making them move.

Amber had kissed her way halfway down my back when Mia said, "Okay, Darcy, it's time to turn over." I had three pairs of hands on my body, helping me roll over, fully exposing myself to the room. I opened my eyes and saw Amber, Olenna, and Mia staring down at me. Amber and Olenna were naked. Off to the right, the manicurist was filming with one of Amber's cameras, and to the left, the pedicurist had the other camera.

"Amber! What the..."

She put a finger on my lips. "Shh, relax. We've got you." She leaned down and kissed me. I let her explore my mouth with her tongue. At the same time, Mia, ever the professional masseuse, placed a warm lavender-scented mask over my eyes and began massaging my left arm, starting at the shoulder and working her way to the elbow. She gripped my forearm and slid her hand to my wrist. The constant pressure on the muscles and tendons caused my fingers to curl. She repeated this several times, then used her powerful thumbs to knead my palm. She moved to my fingers, rolling each joint of each digit between her thumb and forefinger.

The hand massage felt amazing, but it was drowned out by Amber's insistent kissing and fondling of my breasts. She was teasing my nipples into hard buds, stifling my moans with her mouth. I let my right arm fall from the table, and it searched for Amber's pussy, finding it bare and waiting for my fingers. I slid my digits between her labia, and they wiggled inside her, two fingers sliding in on her natural lubricant, my thumb finding her clit. She moaned into my mouth, the vibrations tickling my lips.

Mia laid my arm gently at my side and placed a hand on my sternum, and made her half-circle move around my body, forcing Amber to break the kiss and pull herself away from my hand with a whimper. It was only a moment before she was on my left side. This time, instead of kissing me, she played and sucked on my breasts, dragging her tongue in circles across the areoles and nipping at the nipples. Mia was repeating her process on my right arm.

This entire time, Olenna had been kneading my thigh, her hands repeatedly sliding close to my pussy, sometimes just sliding over it, grazing my hard clit, only to move to the meat of the quadriceps muscles. The sensual teasing aside, she would make a good masseuse.

Mia laid my arm down, and a moment later, her hands found my face, tender fingertips caressing my cheeks, laden with the scent of peppermint. I was surprised when she kissed me, breaking the wall of professionalism, but I eagerly returned the kiss before she broke away. Her voice was huskier than before, and her Spanish accent more pronounced as she whispered, not to me, but to the room in general, "I can't watch this anymore. I have to be a participant." She wiggled a bit, her hands leaving me for a few seconds, then taking my hand and placing it between her legs.

It was the first thick patch of pubic hair I'd felt in a long time. Mia clearly kept it natural. I found her slit and teased my fingers into her. She returned her hands to my body, running them over my stomach and breasts, occasionally intersecting with Amber's. My left hand found Ambers wet pussy again, and she began driving her hips forward onto my fingers.

All these sensations were muted when Olenna finally made her move. She lifted my leg and laid it carefully over her shoulder. She leaned into the space between my legs and kissed my clit, gently at first but sent shockwaves through me. My hips bucked, pressing into her face, and she broke my expected protocol by sliding an oiled finger into my asshole.

It felt like my entire body lifted off the table. The sensation of Olenna's finger sliding so easily past my sphincter was a surprising but welcome sensation. I cried out, but it was muffled by Mia's hungry mouth devouring mine in another passionate kiss.

Olenna pressed her attack, increasing the pace and pressure of her tongue as she danced it around my clit. She was sliding her finger in and out of my ass and added her other hand to the mix, slipping two fingers in my pussy and maneuvering them in the opposite rhythm as the other digit. She'd slide the finger out of my ass and the two into my pussy. It was like her hands were pistons. I felt her fingers passing each other through the wall separating the two pleasure chambers.

I had six hands and three mouths on me. Every orifice had someone's fingers or tongue in it. Both nipples were being stimulated and kept in an aching, hardened state, and I was knuckles deep in two vaginas. All the stimulus was almost overwhelming. Almost.

The internal pressure was building as I crept closer to my orgasm. I heard moaning, and it took a moment to realize it was coming from me. My breathing was rapid, and I could feel my heart beating a furious tempo. My hips were bucking like mad, chasing Olenna's lips and tongue.

Mia lurched and fell on top of me. I felt her pussy convulse around my fingers as she came. She screamed, "Oh fuck! Oh, Jesus," as she thrashed around on me.

That was it. I hit the edge and jumped right off into my own orgasm. I cried out, not even using words but only able to grunt like an animal. Heat washed throughout my body as my pelvic muscles began contracting, and I was no longer in control of my body. I was flotsam in a tempest, my orgasm driving me to the ocean floor and rolling me around before letting me back up for air, but only for a moment. I couldn't stand it, and yet the women kept going, taking me to impossible heights. There was no way I could fight back, not that I wanted to. No resistance I could offer that would end this pleasant torture. Finally, after an eternity spent writhing in ecstasy, Olenna withdrew her hand and lifted her mouth off me. Mia kissed me a few more times, her peppermint lips making mine tingle. While Olenna stood and laid my leg on the table, Mia dutifully resumed the massage, moving from the arm she had been manipulating to my legs. While she kneaded the meat of my quadriceps, I reached up and removed the eye mask. Elena and Amber, both still nude, stood beside the table, smiling. Olenna had her hands on Amber's shoulders and rested her head next to Amber's.

"How do you like Ukrainian massage?" Olenna asked me. She smiled, looking like a wolf fresh from the Carpathian Mountains of her homeland, giving this situation a Red Riding Hood feel, except this Red enjoyed being eaten by the wolf. I tried to speak, but I couldn't form words. I managed to say "good" and offered a thumbs-up, drawing laughter from all three women.

When she finished with my legs, Mia walked along my left side, dragging her fingers along my still sensitive skin, grabbed the thin sheet, and threw it over me. Keeping her voice low, she whispered, "Take a few minutes. Get your bearings. It was a pleasure working on your body."

I nodded and managed to say, "Uh-huh." I looked back at Olenna and Amber and grinned. "So...who goes next?"

Olenna immediately held a fist and against her palm and turned to Amber. "Shall we? Play rock paper scissor?"

Amber held her hands up in the same position. "Best two out of three."

I closed my eyes and listened to fists smacking palms, cries of victory and defeat going back and forth as they battled to be next to receive the Ukrainian massage treatment. I didn't hear who won as I drifted away on a cloud of bliss.

Twenty-Six

Something startled me awake. Was it a door slamming? I was disoriented for a moment in this unfamiliar room. I felt someone lying beside me, and when I lifted my head, I saw Amber and Olenna, sound asleep, draped over each other, and it all clicked into place for me. We were still in Olenna's suite in the Waldorf. After three rounds of Ukrainian massages, Amber and Olenna finished the manicure and pedicure they had started before they'd joined me at the massage table. Olenna had ordered an afternoon tea service, and after they were finished with their spa treatments, we ate finger sandwiches and scones with clotted cream and an assortment of three different kinds of tea.

Amber ran her foot up and down Olenna's leg, prompting the Ukrainian to raise a perfectly sculpted eyebrow. "So... is that bed a California king?"

Olenna grinned her wolf's grin. "The biggest bed there is."

"So...three people will fit on it?"

"Of course. Do you doubt me? Come, I show you proof."

Three hours and multiples of multiple orgasms later, our trio, satiated and exhausted, laid sleeping in a heap together until something woke me up. I quietly rolled out of bed and crept across the room to see what was going on. I cracked the door open and peeked out into the hallway that led to the bedroom. Though I couldn't see his face, the swept-back, greaser style haircut told me it was Gino, or Little Chubby as Gemma had called him. I started out the door to follow him before remembering that I was naked. Cursing, I dug through the clothes we'd thrown into a pile in our haste to get in bed, found my shorts and top, and grabbed my phone from my bag as an afterthought. I pulled the top on as I trotted back to the door and paused to slip my legs into the shorts.

I crept down the hall and saw Gino talking to a huge black man who looked familiar. Of course, I saw him at Club Chubby, but I could not remember his name for the life of me.

"Olenna in there?" the black man asked.

"Yeah, she's been lezzing out again. Has a couple of broads in there with her."

"Damn. I'd love to be able to jump into the middle of that shit."

Gino got indignant. "Watch it, AJ. That's my father's wife. Don't make me regret bringing you instead of your dad!"

Ah! That was it! This was Andre Jr. AJ, the man Ashleigh said lingered too much in the dressing room at the club.

"Sorry, man. I was just making conversation."

"Well, don't. Where's Drago?"

"Who?"

Gino turned toward AJ. I ducked back so he wouldn't see me peeking around the corner.

"Olenna's brother, AJ. Is there another six-and-a-half-foot tall blonde Russian motherfucker you're not telling me about?"

"No, I meant who's Drago. I don't know that name. He's with the Russians?"

"Oh, for fucks... Ivan Drago. Rocky IV? 'I must break you?' Any of this ringing a bell?"

"I never saw that movie, man."

"Fuck me, now I do wish I'd brought your dad. Yuri. Where the fuck is Yuri?"

"Why didn't you just ask that? He's in the bathroom."

"Jesus. That was a long walk for a short drink of water. I'll be in the office."

"Tight. Can I use your bathroom? Since Yuri's got this one tied up...."

"Go, do it. Just run the fan, would you? I don't want you stinking everything up."

I pressed myself as flat as possible as AJ stalked his way down the opposite hallway toward the bedroom Gino occupied. I waited a few seconds and then peeked around the corner. Gino was gone.

I crept out into the main living area, my senses on high alert. Gino was nowhere to be seen, so I looked for a spot in which I could reasonably hide, giving me a view into the room or at least allowing me to hear what was going on. I settled on an area by the kitchenette. I could see part of the office in one direction and see if AJ was coming back from the other, and it was close enough to the refrigerator that I could make a reasonable excuse for my presence.

In the office, I saw his reflection in the window as Gino flipped open a folder and shuffled through some papers. Whatever he was looking at, he didn't like it. "What the fuck is this shit? Those mother fuckers." His reflection grabbed his phone from the desk. "God damn it," he muttered as he pulled his phone out and dialed a number. A few moments passed, and I heard the staccato sound of someone answering, though I couldn't hear what they said.

"Hey, Ira, I just reviewed the paperwork. What is this bullshit? No, that wasn't the deal we had. The deal was ten percent. Right. Yeah, that's right, the building is worth five hundred K, and the land is worth three mil. I've pulled together five hundred thousand in cash. That's four mil, ten percent. No, it wasn't easy. No, I don't have that kind of money lying around. I had to get creative. What do you mean the building doesn't count? Of course, I know we're gonna tear it down. Fuck me. So, I need to come up with another 500 grand. No, god damn it, I'm not asking my father. Because one, he won't give it to me. And B, he'd probably take the business away from me and give it to someone else, and this whole fucking deal goes south. I'll figure something else out. Fucking Christ, Ira, this is the kind of shit you're supposed to be thinking of before they do. No, don't make it my fault. Fuck you, I gotta go back to these fucking shitheads hat in hand and ask for more money, which is exactly the spot I didn't want to be in, goddammit!"

He hung up the phone, closed the folder, and got up from the desk. He headed towards the door to the office, so I scampered over to the fridge to pretend like I was looking for something to eat, but he didn't even look in my direction.

"AJ! Pull up your pants, and let's go!"

Olenna's brother emerged from the bathroom. "What do you need, Gino?"

"I don't need shit from you, Drago."

"My name is Yuri."

"I don't give a fuck." Gino took a breath. "Look, Yuri, I'm sorry. I got bad news on the club deal. I'm pissed, but not at you. You know what you can do? Call the valet and have them bring the car around."

Yuri hustled to the phone on the living room table while Gino walked to the hallway leading to his bedroom. "AJ! Come on, let's GO!"

I may as well have been invisible as AJ rushed from the bedroom and hustled to the door with Gino. Yuri walked after them and called out, "Car is on its way!"

I took the chance while all their backs were to me to scurry into the office. I wanted to get a look at what was in that folder. I glanced up to ensure no one was coming and turned my focus to it.

It was branded across the top with an address. I recognized it because I'd recently put that address in Waze when Gemma and I went to meet Ashleigh; it was the address of Club Chubby. "What are you up to, Gino?"

I flipped the cover open and saw a bunch of legalese and real estate mumbo jumbo underneath a picture of the strip club. Scanning through a few lines, I realized it was an appraisal of the building, and the land, on which it sat. I took a picture with my phone, noticing the battery was down to five percent. *Fuck.* I flipped through several pages of

219

risk assessments and market analyses. Then I came to the sheet with a picture, under which was written 'artist's rendering.' It was a three-story building with shops on the main floor and what looked like apartments with balconies on the next two. Several addresses were written on this section of the documentation. It was the address of Club Chubby and the addresses for the businesses on either side. Businesses which I knew from our visit last week were currently boarded up. I snapped another picture.

Gino was going to take over his father's business, tear it down, and build condos in its place.

I was so focused on the file I didn't hear the footsteps headed toward the office until it was too late. With nowhere to go, I flipped the folder shut and crawled under the desk. *Jesus, what a cliché!*

Heavy, hurried footsteps pushed into the carpet. As they sped their way toward me, I took a deep breath and held it so I wouldn't make any noise. A pair of thick men's legs appeared in front of me. I heard him shuffling papers on the desk for a moment, then the legs turned and headed back the way they came. Just as I started to relax, the figure was back, crouched down in front of the opening, staring at me.

It was Olenna's brother, Yuri. He laughed and spoke in his thick Ukrainian accent – much thicker than Olenna's—"Gino won't be back for long time, Leetle Bird. If you want blow him, come back later." He smiled, showing off the gold premolar on the upper right side of his mouth. "If you want blow *me*, I'll be right back."

My mind scrambled, looking for a response. I settled on, "Okay. Thanks. I'll come back. Don't tell Gino I was in here, okay? This was supposed to be a surprise."

"Your secret's safe with me, Leetle Bird." He held out his large hand and helped me out from under the desk, and he left with the stack of papers I had been leafing through.

As Yuri headed to the suite's entrance, I assumed to take the papers to Gino. I veered to the left, down the hallway to Olenna's room, and burst through the door, startling both Amber and Olenna awake.

"What is problem?" Olenna asked through a stretch.

I started grabbing Amber's clothes and throwing them at her. "Nothing's wrong, Olenna. We just need to go. We're late, and our boss is pissed."

Amber hadn't caught on yet. "Wait, Ruby? What boss? Tawney? She doesn't care. Neither of us is on cam tonight."

"She had that meeting tonight, remember? And we had chores to do beforehand?"

"Ruby, I don't...." Amber paused, a look of recognition crossing her face. "Oh, shit, you're right! That's *tonight.*" She gave me a wink and began putting on her clothes while I gathered the video equipment.

Olenna seemed put out at our sudden preparations for departure. "I guess I'll have Yuri drive you back to your car then."

I walked over to the side of the bed. "Olenna, thank you for everything today. I appreciate the rescue, and the massage, and the...."

"Look, we had fun afternoon. Don't make more of it than it is. Go, fly, birdies. I'll get Yuri to drive you."

"We'll get an Uber," Amber chimed in from the foot of the bed. "It's no trouble, really."

"Whatever. Have nice meeting with your boss."

We hurried from the room, and once we were a safe distance away from the door, Amber pulled me close and hissed in my ear. "What is this all about?"

"I'll tell you in the elevator. Let's just get out of here."

We hustled to the suite's entrance and pulled the door open to find another of Gino's security guards reaching for the handle. He was dark-haired and at least six inches shorter than Yuri, but his accent was similar. This must be Oleg.

"Well! Just who I was looking for!" His tone was menacing, and he made no attempt to hide it. "Gino would like word with you. It seems you had nice peek inside folder, and he'd like to know why."

Fucking Yuri. Way to keep my secret! "I have no idea what you're talking about. Excuse us." I tried to move past him, but he was twice as wide as me and infinitely stronger. His hand encircled my arm with plenty of overlap. He yanked me back in front of him.

"I don't think so, *bitch*!" Pronounced *beetch*.

I heard Amber grunt and the sound of flesh pounding flesh. He released my arm, and I looked up to see him clutching his throat, a gurgle escaping his lips. She raised a leg, almost Karate Kid-style, and snapped her foot into his groin. As he doubled over, she used his momentum and yanked him forward, sending him crown-first into the door, his head making a satisfying 'thunk' on the solid core.

I looked at Amber in awe. "You just chopped down an oak tree!"

"Krav Maga. Come on, he won't be down for long, and I won't catch him off guard a second time." She pulled my arm and led me to the elevator. Once there, she hit the button and pulled out her phone. "There's a rideshare stand outside. Hopefully, there's a car waiting, and we won't have to stand there waiting for the brute squad to snatch us."

She messed with her phone while waiting for the elevator, getting the confirmation just as the doors opened. We stepped inside, and I hit the button for the lobby a dozen times as if that would make the doors close faster.

"Excellent. Brian will meet us in his black Nissan Altima." She turned to me. "Now, are you going to tell me what the fuck is going on? What games are you playing, Ruby, if that's even your real name."

"You know it's not my real name."

"Whatever. Just tell me why I had to groin a dude up there."

"Okay, I'll tell you, but I don't have all the facts yet."

"Well then, tell me what you do know."

The elevator doors opened, and we made a beeline for the entrance. Halfway through the lobby, we passed Gino, AJ, and Yuri.

"Hey, there they are!" Gino pointed at us as we hustled past. "Don't just stand there. Get them!" He slapped each of the guards on the shoulder to get them moving.

The two huge men started after us. In a scene from a cheesy action flick, AJ got entangled in an old Japanese couple's luggage, and after three or four lumbering, stumbling strides, he finally succumbed to gravity and hit the marble floor with a loud *smack*.

That just left Yuri, Olenna's hulking Ukrainian brother, still in hot pursuit. What was his endgame here? Surely he didn't think he was going to grab two women and force them against their will back into the hotel, did he? In front of literally dozens of witnesses?

It seemed like that was precisely his plan as we passed through the large brass-framed doors at the entrance to the hotel. The doormen opened the doors wide for us, and we dashed through to the transportation queue outside. While Amber looked for our ride, I looked back at Yuri, who was surprisingly close to us.

He spoke in a hurried, accented whispering shout. "Struggle, then kick balls. It's okay. Olenna told me watch over you."

"Ruby! Let's go; our ride's here!"

I nodded at Amber and turned back to Yuri. "You're sure?"

"Yes, do it."

HA Blackwood

"Get off me, you fucking jerk!" I screamed at him, then whispered, "sorry, but you should have kept my secret!"

"Papers were out of order! Now kick!"

I swung my leg and kicked him in the groin harder than I needed or even intended to. He folded, clutching at his crotch. "Shit! Yuri, I didn't mean.."

"Go!" He grunted through a red face. I felt terrible as I sprinted to the black Altima. I slid into the back seat next to Amber, pulling the door shut behind me.

Amber leaned forward. "Brian, go. There's a big tip for you if you get us there fast."

He turned and smiled. "Lady—"

"Amber."

"Amber, I'm not going to get a ticket for you. You know as well as I do we're at the mercy of LA traffic."

"It's three miles. A hundred bucks."

"A hundred bucks won't even cover the ticket these greedy mother fuckin' cops will write me if I try and perpetrate a fast ride."

Amber sighed. "I'll show you my tits."

Brian did a quick double-take. "Say what? For real?"

She smiled and nodded.

"Fuck it then. Deal."

She pulled her tube top down, showing our driver her D-cups, and shimmied her shoulders a little to get her breasts swaying. Brian's eyes bugged out at her display. She pulled the top back up. "Okay, Brian, step on the gas."

Brian stepped on the gas, whipping out of the entryway. "God damn, I love LA. I've been here two months, and this is the ninth time that's happened to me."

Amber rolled her eyes and turned to me. "Okay, Ruby. Spill."

I debated how much to tell her. Should she know that I was undercover? How else could I explain everything I knew? I opted to tell her a version of the truth, but not the whole truth. "Okay. Short version? The guy Olenna is here with is behind the missing money."

Amber's mouth hung open for a second before she regained her composure. "You're kidding me, right? Are you telling me we just spent the afternoon with – getting *fucked* by the person who's been fucking us out of our money too?"

I saw Brian look in the rearview, his eyebrows raised. I tuned him out. "I don't know if Olenna knows what is going on."

"Oh, come on, Ruby. She's here with him. Of course, she knows."

"I'm not so sure. Olenna's not *with* this guy; she's married to his father. And the deal he has cooking is probably going to piss daddy off."

"So, how do you know he's behind the missing money?"

"I heard part of a conversation this morning, and the amounts discussed were remarkably similar."

"But you didn't hear him say 'I took the money,' right?"

"No."

"Well, there's a lot of supposition there. We're going to need more evidence than 'I overheard one side of a conversation' if we're going to get the police to take us seriously."

"Agreed, but since he had Grabby the Goon manhandling us at the hotel—"

"Manhandling *you,* you mean. I saved your ass."

"Yeah, yeah. Anyway, I think since Gino was ready to kidnap us, it's a pretty good signal he knows that we know."

"Yeah, but still, that's not enough for the cops. They've been dicks to us about this whole thing."

"Amber, now we have a name, and we have a motive. It's going to be enough to get them to look into him."

Brian interrupted them. "Hey, uh, ladies? These people y'all talking about that's doing all the robbing and kidnapping and killing...."

"They've not killed anyone. That I know of," I corrected him.

"Yeah, well, if that's them behind us, I think they want to. Black SUV, big Russian-looking mother fucker behind the wheel."

We both turned and looked behind us. Sure enough, Yuri was driving the SUV with Gino in the passenger seat. I noticed the passenger side turn signal and the front part of the fender we smashed in. "He's not Russian. He's Ukrainian," I explained.

"As if that helps! I trust those beefy mother fuckers even less! And I'm sorry if my language offends you, but you gonna need to give a lot more than a look at them titties if Ivan Drago back there does some Ukrainian shit and fucks up my car, or worse, *me*." I chuckled that everyone called Yuri 'Drago.'

Amber was messing with her phone. "Brian, I changed the destination. We can't go to my car because we'll never get away from them."

Brian fiddled with the phone attached to the magnetic mount on his dashboard. "Oh, okay, you want to really test my skill navigating this mother fucker through West Hollywood, huh?"

I rolled my eyes at Amber. "Okay, Samuel Jackson, just get us there, alright?"

Brian looked at me in the rear-view mirror. "It's how I respond to stress, alright? And if I get killed or something, your rider rating is gonna suffer, Amber. Fuck!"

The light at the next intersection turned red, forcing Brian to stop. I looked back, and sure enough, Gino was climbing out of the SUV and heading our way.

"Hey Brian, run this light, and you not only get to see them, but you can touch my tits," Amber said.

"For real?"

"For real. But we have to get to the house first, big Bri."

He looked both ways at North Beverly Drive, checking cross traffic, and let the Altima roll forward into the crosswalk. I glanced back at Gino. A pissed-off look crossed his face, and he started to trot after us. Just as I was about to say something to Brian, he hit the gas, lurching me into the seat.

Cars honked at us as we weaved our way through the intersection. Brian had a massive grin on his face. "Oh, it's on, now! You Russian motha fuckaaaaas got nothing on Brian James!"

He made a hard left on North Crescent, then a right on Clifton.

"Yeeeeah!" He continued gloating. "You think you know this town better than me? No chance, Ivan! West Hollywood is *my* town! WeHo good to *go*!"

Brian made a left onto Foothill Rd, and after a few stop signs and a jog over Civic Center Drive, we found ourselves on Santa Monica Boulevard. I looked over at Amber, who simply shrugged. "How long did you say you've been here, Brian?"

He looked at me in the mirror. "Two months. Twelve hours a day, seven days a week, navigating the mean streets of West Hollywood." He cut around a slow-moving Mercedes. The stoplight at Doheny turned yellow, and Brian put his foot on the gas, skating into the intersection just as the light turned red. "Whooo! Can't stop a mother fucker!!"

We continued on for a half-mile to San Vicente and made a left, then after another half-mile, we turned right on Sunset Boulevard and a few blocks later made the left onto Sunset Plaza Drive, heading into the canyon. Amber and I both breathed a sigh of relief. There was no sign of the black SUV, and we were just a couple minutes from the house.

Brian wound his way up the canyon road, did not miss the turn as my previous Uber driver had, and a minute later, dropped us off at the house.

I slid out of the rear passenger side door. I turned to offer a hand to Amber, but she waved me off. "I have to let Speed Racer here feel me up. A deal's a deal."

I nodded as she climbed into the front seat next to a massively grinning Brian. Shaking my head, I turned and trotted into the house.

Twenty-Seven

Tawney and Gemma were on me the second I walked in the door.

"Thank Christ, you're all right!" Gemma grabbed and hugged me, going perilously close to breaking our cover.

Tawney must have sensed this because she broke in and gave me the same hug. "Where's Amber?"

"She's, uh, taking care of the driver." Gemma and Tawney traded confused glances. I shook my head. "Never mind. Let's get to the office so we can talk freely."

Tawney let go of me and waved her arm in a grandiose fashion. "Proceed, ma'am."

Gemma brought up the rear and pulled the sliding door shut. I was already sitting in a chair by the computer when Gemma got in, and she was angry.

"Okay, Darcy—"

"Ruby," Tawney corrected.

"Whatever. Tell us what's going on! We got a cryptic text from Amber about Ukrainian gangsters. What happened today?"

"Okay, short version: Little Chub is behind everything."

Gemma was incredulous. "What? Gino isn't smart enough to pull this off. At least, I don't think he is."

"Well, I have some evidence, if my phone was charged." I searched for the ever-present charging cable plugged into the Obi-Tech charger. I found it and plugged my phone in. When I saw the red low battery symbol pop up, indicating it was charging, I set it on the desk. "Okay, here's the deal. Gemma, remember when we went to Club Chubby?"

"Yeah, of course."

"And the buildings all around it were shuttered?"

"Yeah. We just figured it's been a tough economy."

"Well, that's not it, not entirely. Gino has been buying the buildings and leaving them empty. He's going to tear them all down and put up a condo complex. The only building standing in his way is—"

"Club Chubby, which he's about to inherit." Gemma finished my thought. "That crafty son-of-a-bitch."

"What does this have to do with our stolen money?" Tawney asked.

"I overheard a call, and I have pictures on my phone of some of the financials of his deal. He was pissed – he said the amounts were different than what they had discussed. He'd already given them money, and now they were asking for more. The numbers he was throwing around seemed really similar to what we talked about here."

Gemma nodded along with what I was saying. "So he steals the money from Tawney and XX Cam to finance the deal. But how did he know how to hit them?"

"Mercedes," Tawney said. "She had to tell him. This started happening right before she left for that club."

"Seems right, but how would she know the passwords after you changed them? She left, and you've changed passwords on the accounts several times."

"Yeah, that's puzzling," Tawney conceded, "But, it has to be her, right? I don't believe in coincidences."

My phone buzzed, indicating that it was charged enough to power on. I grabbed it, but the cable was tangled, and I pulled the charger out of the socket. It flew past me, across the narrow room, hit the wall on the opposite side, and broke into a half dozen pieces. "Oh, shit! I'm sorry!"

I knelt down to pick up the pieces. I gathered them, hoping I could snap them together. As I turned the parts over in my hands, I was hit by a thunderbolt. "Holy fucking shit!"

Tawney waved her hand toward the trash can under the desk. "It's not a big deal. Just toss it, Ruby. We've got a bunch of them laying around."

I held out one piece of the charger. "A bunch like this? With a freaking *camera* inside it?"

Her eyes went wide. She and Gemma, at the same time, exclaimed, "What!?"

I held it out to Tawney. "See for yourself. This is a spy cam."

Gemma said out loud what we were all realizing. "Whoever had access to that was able to see the keyboard and capture the password every time you changed it."

Tawney's face devolved into a scowl.

I put a hand on her leg. "What is it, Tawney?"

"Amber. She had a bunch of these. Handed them out to everyone."

Gemma leaned forward. "When?"

"Right about the time the money started going missing. A little bit before, actually."

"Do you think she'd..." I started, but Tawney cut me off.

"I don't want to think any of my girls would do this. But here we are. And she did hand out those chargers to everyone."

Gemma cleared her throat. "Okay, Tawney, change all your account passwords right now. We can look at the PC later and see how the video was being sent and where to. It might help us pinpoint who is behind this." She turned to me. "Go get Amber."

Twenty-Eight

I found Amber walking up to the door, smiling.

"Brian is actually a really funny guy! He's reading for a part in a Ron Howard film next week!"

She took a few more steps before the look on my face registered with her, and her smile faded, replaced with concern.

"What is it, Ruby? What's happened?"

"Look... just come with me, okay?"

"Not until you tell me what's going on!"

"We think we know how the money got stolen."

Her face brightened. "Well, that's great! Can we connect it to the thugs that were chasing us?"

I would not have expected Amber to be excited about this turn of events if she was the one who was behind the spy camera. "Well, come on. You're going to want to see this."

She fell in behind me as I headed back into the house and into Tawney's office. We found Tawney and Gemma waiting for us, serious mean bitch looks on their faces.

Amber looked confused again. "What's going on? Why do you all look like someone died?"

Gemma tossed the pieces of the spycam charger to her. "What do you know about this?"

"I didn't break it!" The defensive tone in her voice sounded genuine. "I have like, a dozen of them. I can get you another one if you want."

Tawney nodded. "Yeah, I remember you passing them out to people. Where did you get them?"

"Mercedes left them behind when she left. She got them from...."

We all waited a few seconds after she trailed off. When she didn't continue, I prodded her. "Amber, what is it?"

"I... that man from today?"

"Gino?"

"Yes. He was here in December." She looked at Tawney. "Remember? We had that party. He was here with some people from the strip club in Colorado, the one Mercedes went to. I didn't make that connection until just now. They gave her a box of these chargers. But what's the big deal? How does this tie into the stolen money?"

Tawney nodded and turned to Gemma and me. "We had an industry party. Lots of people in and out that night. It's possible."

Gemma was unconvinced. "I can't believe that Ashleigh—Mercedes—would do this, though. She had as much to lose as anyone."

"Except she left to the very club that Gino runs now."

"Yeah, Tawney, but she's working the pole. That's a pay cut from what you guys have going here. Why would she do that?"

Tawney gestured at the computer. "You think he's not giving her a kickback from the stolen money? Maybe even a cut of the real estate deal he's cooking up? I'm sure he made it worth her while."

"Okay, that makes sense," Gemma conceded. "It's just inconsistent with the woman I knew."

Everyone was quiet for a moment until Amber broke the silence. "What does a phone charger have to do with the stolen money?"

I pointed to the lens in the broken piece of phone charger in her hand. "It's a remote-control camera. It was positioned where whoever was watching could see the keyboard and the screen."

Her mouth dropped open. "Camera? Fuck! I have one by my bed! Mother fucker!" She tossed the broken pieces to Gemma and fled the office, running to the room that, for the moment, I shared with her.

I looked at Gemma. "What now?"

"I'm going to take a look at the computer and see what it tells me about this camera. If we can figure out where it's sending the money to, we go to the cops, and we hope the money is still there."

Tawney shook her head. "I'll get Maya and Freya. They can find it in there faster than you."

She left to find her tech team, and Gemma sat in the chair in front of the PC. "I can't believe Ashleigh would be involved in this."

"You don't want to believe it. But it might be true. You need to prepare for that possibility."

"I know. But, it's just... It's not like her. You saw the shape she's in. She's put a lot of work into this move. Why do all that if you're getting a fat payout?"

"You're the finance wizard, Gem. It's not like they've stolen millions. Even if they gave her ten percent, that's like one year's average salary. She still has to work."

Gemma pursed her lips. "Yeah. I guess, but then the club is getting shut down, so she's still out of a job. It makes no sense any way you slice it. Fuck! I hate this."

I put a hand on her shoulder, and she grabbed it and kissed it. "I know, baby. But the evidence goes where it goes."

She let out a long sigh, still holding onto my hand. "I know. I'm going to hate it, but I know."

Tawney returned with the two goth tech specialists. Freya walked over and motioned for Gemma to get out of the chair. "Now that we know what we're looking for, this should be easy."

Twenty-Nine

"Got it!"

Freya worked on the PC for less than fifteen minutes and located the information we were looking for. Tawney leaped from her chair and rushed to the woman's side.

"You found the IP address where the videos were going?"

"Yes. Well, a lot more than that. I got the email address. It's a Gmail account, but the..." she could see everyone's eyes glazing over. "Well, there's a log of each email, which includes not just the receiving IP address, but the machine address that opened it. In other words, there's enough information here for the police to know the exact PC, laptop, tablet, or phone that opened each email. There are several, but two that come up the most."

She opened a browser tab, went to a search site, put in one IP, and then the second one. "One of them is a mobile phone. The other is an IP from Colorado. I know the internet service provider and the phone company, but I can't get more information from here, like the owners of the accounts or the addresses. I'll send it to some people I know. They'll be able to get us that info, maybe faster than the police."

"Why didn't you find this before?" Gemma asked.

Maya spoke up. "We didn't know we were looking for a camera or video files before. We assumed it was a keylogger—a virus that records your keystrokes—so we were looking for something completely different."

Freya nodded. "Yes, and the code that was installed is clever – it's added into the code for the PC's camera protocol. That's where I found the email subroutine. A virus check would never find it. And the camera is Bluetooth connected but shows up as 'speaker' in the device listing. Since you have Bluetooth speakers, it didn't seem out of place. It's really kind of clever in its simplicity."

"It's almost hiding in plain sight," Maya added.

Tawney picked up her phone and flipped through her contacts. "I'm calling the detective in charge of the case. Now that we have some good evidence, they have to proceed with it."

"It won't be that easy. With multiple jurisdictions and states involved, I bet they're going to have to involve the feds," Gemma speculated.

Tawney's call connected. "Hello? Yes, detective Jimenez please?" She covered the microphone. "They already have. It's wire fraud or something like that."

Gemma smiled. "Good. That will help things move faster if they've already connected the different agencies."

Freya pushed back from the desk. "I've emailed you the information, along with details of what exactly I found and where I found it. You know they're going to want to take the PC for evidence, though, right?"

Tawney shrugged. "Yeah, I figured. I can get another one easy enough." She held a finger up. "Yes, detective? This is Tawney Darling with XX Cam. I have new information about who's been stealing our money."

Thirty

Amber was sitting with her legs crossed on her bed, looking over at me. "I gathered up all the chargers from all the girls and smashed them with a hammer."

"All of them? I kinda wanted to see one. See how it works."

Someone knocked on our door. Amber called out, "Come in!"

Luna opened the door and held out two of the black USB chargers. "Diamond said you were collecting these? They really have cameras in them?"

"They do. I've been smashing them all. Give one to Ruby though, she said she wanted to figure out how they work."

Luna tossed one to Amber and one to me. "You think whoever is behind this thing was watching all of us with these? It's creepy as fuck to think about."

I shook my head. "I don't think so. From what I got from Freya and Maya, the camera has to connect to a PC or Bluetooth to be active and send video. And she only found evidence on Tawney's PC of the one camera being active."

"Huh. One was enough, though, wasn't it? She's going to the cops again, yeah?"

"They're coming out right now. Bringing their tech guy."

Amber snorted. "Yeah. So Freya can show him how to do his job."

Luna laughed. "Right? They could do a lot worse than hiring her as a consultant. Be cheaper for them, and she'd make more coin."

"Yeah!" Amber agreed. "There's probably a TV show in there somewhere. Like Psyche, but with tech instead of a psychic."

While Amber and Luna kept talking about a fictitious TV show starring two goth tech-savvy women consulting with the West Hollywood Police Department, I plugged the charger into a socket and opened my Bluetooth settings. A new device called "speaker" was available. I connected to it, and my phone went through its machinations for a minute. A message popped up.

Device Speaker would like to access the internet. Allow Deny

I clicked allow, and it opened a website. Much of the writing was in a language I didn't recognize. Another window popped up.

Your viewing link is ready. Please bookmark or share.

I closed the message and there, on the screen, was a view from the charger across the room. I copied the link and texted it to Amber.

She stopped in mid-sentence, halting the conversation she was having with Luna to look at her screen. "What is this, Ruby?"

"Just click it and let me know what happens."

Luna leaned over and watched as the website loaded, and a second later, both of them gasped.

"Holy fuck! That's us!" Luna exclaimed.

"And so fast!" Amber agreed. "And look – you can record it, download the video, send it to whoever. Holy shit, this is scary!"

"Okay, now let me know what happens."

I shut my phone down and waited for her to react. It didn't take long.

"I just got a pop-up message that says the video link has been severed. Would I like to be notified when it starts transmitting again?"

"Say yes. My phone is already restarting."

We waited another thirty seconds while my phone started up and reconnected all the data, WiFi, and Bluetooth connections. A minute later, Amber's phone chimed.

"I got an alert! 'Your video stream is now online.' Should I click it?"

"Yes!" Luna and I both said at once.

Amber clicked the link and, a second later, exclaimed, "It's back!"

I went to the Bluetooth connections and deleted "speaker" from the list.

Amber said, "And it's gone again."

I smiled. "Well, now we know how the cameras work. You have to have an active connection to the camera for it to stream."

Luna knitted her brows. "So, that means what? No one was watching us?"

"Right, I don't think so. Unless any of the girls connected to the camera by accident and clicked through all the setup instructions, I don't think anyone was watching."

I saw her shoulders relax. "Good, that makes me feel better. Talk to you later. I have to get ready for my show tonight."

Luna closed the door behind her as she left. Amber looked over at me. "You probably think it's weird, right? We make our living exposing ourselves on camera, but we're freaked out by these spy cams."

"No, I get it. It freaks me the fuck out to think that someone has eyes on me in my own room without my knowledge or permission. It's creepy as hell!

"But, about the difference? For me, it's about consent and privacy. One you do willingly, on your terms, and the other is stolen from you. It's a violation."

She nodded. "Yeah, you get it. Now, give me that one. I'm going to smash it and this one. I want them out of this house."

Thirty-One

The detective was already in the office when I walked in. Gemma made introductions.

"Detective Jimenez, this is Darcy Ford. Here in the house, she goes by Ruby. Darcy, this is Detective Jimenez and his electronic forensic team, John Sheldon and Jamie Gerts."

I perked up at Jamie Gerts' name, but before I could say anything, she said, "It's spelled differently."

I smiled. "You get that a lot, huh?"

"Here? In Hollywood? Only all the time."

Detective Jimenez uncrossed his arms to shake my hand, then recrossed them, resuming his stern glare at the monitor while Sheldon and Gerts chatted about what they were finding.

"Do you understand all the tech speak?" I asked him.

He looked at me sideways, without completely turning his head, peering over the top of his glasses. "No, not really. That's why we have the nerds on the payroll." He said it affectionately, bringing smiles to their faces.

"Nerds that help solve half your cases," Sheldon said. "And this one is no different."

Jimenez's face lit up. "Yeah, what have you got?"

Sheldon flipped his laptop around. "The IPs all go to Colorado, and the ISP and Mobile all belong to the same entity. Poppa Chubby's Gentlemen's Club, LLC."

Gemma spat the words out. "So it *is* Gino!"

Sheldon furrowed his brow. "Is he the owner of the club?"

"He will be very soon."

"Well, if it's him, he has help, unless he's been using two different PCs and two different mobile phones. We have four MAC addresses in here for devices registered to that company. Plus, several others have no owner listed. Burners, basically untraceable."

I spoke up this time, thinking about Oleg. "He's got personal security which probably helps him, or he uses their phones."

"Well, until we can put the phones in the hands of someone, it's going to be hard to prove who actually conducted these transactions since the phones aren't registered to individuals."

Tawney was shocked. "You mean with all this information, we still can't go after them? What the fuck...."

Jimenez interrupted her. "Ms. Darling, that's not what he's saying. We'll go after this, but it's harder. This Little Chub? Is that his name? Can simply say he was unaware of any illegal activity and blame it on the staff. And then which staff members? They'll all deny it, and if these devices are pooled resources, checked out by anyone who works there, it would provide plenty of reasonable doubt. So, it's like we have a smoking gun but can't prove who was holding it. Make sense?"

Tawney nodded.

"So we have to go at this from a different angle. Try to find someone we know is involved but not at the top level. Someone who would roll over and finger the ones who actually committed the crimes to save their skin."

Gemma and I looked at each other and, at the same time, said, "Ashleigh."

Thirty-Two

We pulled into the parking lot and drove around the rear to the employee parking.

"There's her car. The pink Carmen Ghia." Gemma pointed at the faded pink Porsche knock-off.

I adjusted the microphone under my bra and held up my phone on speaker. "Okay, so we're supposed to get her to confess involvement, get out, and you guys pick her up at home later and get her to flip. That sum it up?"

Detective Jimenez sat in a conference room at the Jefferson County Sheriff's Department on the other end of the call. The Lakewood Police Department wasn't too keen on getting involved with the case due to all the different jurisdictions involved and pawned it off on the Sheriff's Department, saying the business and the people involved were in other cities but were all in Jefferson County. The JeffCo Sheriff, for his part, was on board right away.

The deputy assigned to the case, Murdock, set us up with the wires we were wearing. "Yep. That's all we need."

Jimenez chimed in. "And be careful. Remember those aren't transmitters, so if you get into trouble, you need to get out."

"Yeah," Gemma said, "And why is that?"

We heard Murdock chuckle. "We don't have all the equipment that every department on TV has. Just get her to admit she's complicit and get out, and we'll handle the rest."

"Okay, got it." I hung up the phone and looked at Gemma. "You ready for this?"

She took a minute, staring at the steering wheel, nodding her head absently. "Yeah. Yeah, I am. Let's go."

She dialed a number, and I heard a voice say something, but I couldn't tell what it was. "Hey. Yeah, we're here. Wanna let us in? Yup, right by your Ghia. Okay, thanks!" She turned to me. "Let's go."

We got out of the car and walked over to the employee entrance, and by the time we got there, Mercedes was holding the door open for us. She was smiling a broad grin.

"Hey, ladies! I was glad to hear from you! You have to tell me everything you found out!"

We walked in and followed her to her station. I eyed the black phone charger plugged into the outlet over her counter.

"So," she said as she sat down, "tell me what you guys found out!"

Gemma pulled up a chair, and I did the same. Gemma went first. "Well, we figured out how they were getting access to the accounts. And we have a good idea who it was that was doing it."

Ashleigh smiled broadly. "You did! Awesome! Did you tell the police?"

Like Amber back in L.A., she certainly wasn't acting like someone involved with the crimes we were discussing.

"Yeah, we did. They're following up on leads now."'

Ashleigh pressed for more info. "So, how were they doing it? Was it a virus? Did they hack Tawney's PC?"

Gemma started laying the trap. "No, it was a spy camera."

Ashleigh looked genuinely surprised. "A spy camera? What do you mean?"

"A spy camera, built into the phone charger Tawney was using."

"How the fuck did she get a charger with a spy cam in it? That seems really random."

Gemma nodded. "You'd think so. But it's not so random when everyone in the entire house had them."

Ashleigh furrowed her brow. "Everyone had one? How the..." An expression of recognition crossed her face. "You mean the ones I gave them?"

Gemma just stared at her.

"You don't think I was the one stealing from them? What the fuck, Gemma? I'm the one who told you about this! Why would I do that if I was behind it?"

"I don't know, Ashleigh. I don't think you stole the money. I don't want to think you had anything to do with this. But you did supply the equipment that was used to steal it. Even if all you did was help set up that camera, you're going to go down with everyone."

Ashleigh was indignant. "How can you even think I'd have anything to do with this? You know me, Gemma! What the fuck?"

"The chargers had cameras in them, Ashleigh. And you passed them out to everyone, even left the extras with Amber. It'd be a pretty big coincidence if you had nothing to do with it, don't you think? I mean, that's how the police are looking at it. I don't want to believe it, baby, believe me. But the evidence is there. If someone pressured you into it, you could tell the police, and they'll give you a deal."

"I wasn't pressured to do anything! Andre gave me the chargers at the Christmas party. He told me they were high-speed chargers and way better for our phones. Said it was a gift from Club Chubby to the girls of XX Cam. So I went around and gave them to everyone. Including Tawney. I had no fucking idea they had cameras in them!"

"I'm sorry. Did I hear my name?"

Gemma and I spun around and found ourselves facing Andre.

Ashleigh spilled our secret to him. "Andre, did you know the phone chargers you had me give to the girls at Christmas had spy cameras in them? That's how the people stealing the money from XX Cam knew the passwords to the bank accounts! The cops think I had something to do with it!"

Andre moved closer. "Do the cops know I gave them to you to pass out?"

Ashleigh looked at Gemma and me. "Do they?"

Neither of us said anything. Andre was impatient, and his tone was menacing. "Think very carefully. Do the police know she got the chargers from me?"

I bluffed. "No. We didn't know that until Ashleigh just told us."

Andre spoke into a walkie-talkie. "AJ, bring the car around back." He turned back to us. "That's good. That's really good."

Gemma asked the question we were all thinking. "Did you know there were cameras in them? Where did you get them? If you did it because Gino asked you to, you could tell the cops what he asked you to do. It'll get you out of the hot seat."

He gestured at me. "You. Red, put your phone down."

I looked at him, trying to keep my face neutral. "Um, no, I don't think I will."

He pulled a gun from his waistband. "I think you will. AJ just missed you with the SUV in Beverly Hills. I won't miss with this pistol. Don't make me ask again."

My blood ran cold, and my hand was shaking as I remembered the close call with the black SUV on Rodeo Drive. I sat my phone on the counter. He gestured with the gun at Gemma. "Put yours on the counter too, please, Alexis."

Gemma seemed a lot cooler than I was as she sat her phone next to mine. "Andre, this isn't like you! Stop it; this makes you seem really guilty. Please, you can roll over on Gino. You don't have to point a gun at us. Don't protect him out of some misguided sense of loyalty. You said yourself he probably won't keep you on once he takes over. You don't think he'll let you take the blame for all of this?"

"Baby girl, you think Gino was behind this? He's too busy trying to close this place down to do something like this."

That surprised me. "You knew about that?"

Andre snorted. "Yeah, I knew. He talked about it all the time in front of me. I think he thought I was too stupid to piece together what he was doing. And me, AJ, and the rest of the people who work here were going to be out on the street. I can't afford that! I got mouths to feed! When he asked me to come with him to LA last summer, we had lunch with Ashleigh. She told us about how much money XX Cam was making. That stuck in my head. She gave us a tour of the house and mentioned the computer center being, and I quote, 'the hub of the operation.' That stuck in my head too. So when Gino asked me to come out again in December, I got the idea of hacking them and taking some of the loads of money Ashleigh said they had laying around."

Gemma kept him talking. "So Ashleigh had nothing to do with it? And neither did Gino?"

He shook his head. "It was all me. The big, dumb, strip club doorman."

"How did you get the cameras?"

"That was AJ. He has some connections. Electronic crime is the wave of the future. You don't have to leave the house, face dogs, angry armed homeowners, none of that."

AJ walked in from the back door. "Hey, Dad, got the car right out back."

Andre gestured toward the employee entrance. "Okay, ladies. Time to take a ride."

Ashleigh was near panic. "Andre, what the fuck? What are you going to do?"

"Yeah, Pops, what are we doing?" AJ asked.

"Well, we ain't fucking going to jail, that's for sure, son. Just do what I say." He gestured at us again. "Now get up and start walking. It's a lot easier than dragging you out of here."

Thirty-Three

We walked single file, following AJ, with Andre Sr behind us with the gun. I wracked my brain for a solution. My only thought was to make a sprint for the road the second we hit the outside and hope that Gemma was on the same page.

Andre grabbed Ashleigh's hair and pulled her close to him. "When we get outside, you ladies are going to climb in the back of the SUV. Try anything funny, and I'll just kill baby girl here on the spot. You understand? I wanna hear 'yes, sir' from you."

"Yes, sir," Gemma and I replied in unison.

AJ opened the door and looked around. Satisfied, he went and opened the back door on the GMC Yukon, and Gemma slid in, followed by me.

"AJ, you ride in the back row. Baby girl, you ride shotgun."

AJ climbed in and hopped onto the third-row bench. Ashleigh got in the front seat while Dre got behind the steering wheel and started the engine.

"I'm really sorry about this, girls. I wish that you hadn't come here asking questions. We were going to be gone in a few days, and all of this could have been avoided."

Gemma again kept him talking; I assumed to get it on tape. Though, the odds of anyone hearing the recording now seemed to be getting more and more remote. "Where were you going? And on four hundred thousand? That's not enough to disappear on."

Andre laughed. "You think this was the only scam we had working? Once we got this going with XX Cam, we got several more in the works. We have over a million stashed right now, and the last hit was going to be Club Chubby's accounts. Both the main ones and Little Chub's private ones. You can live really cheap in Belize for a long time on the kind of money we have. Now we just have to step up our plans a few days."

He put the SUV in gear and pulled out onto the street, made a left, and headed toward the interstate. The light turned red at the corner, and we stopped. An SUV pulled up behind us, and others turned from the cross street, heading straight toward the front of ours. It seemed like dozens of men wearing helmets and vests with "SHERIFF" emblazoned on them, carrying machine guns poured out of the three vehicles, guns trained on Andre. At least, I hope they were all trained on Andre.

They pulled the doors open, and Ashleigh, Gemma, and I were pulled out of the Yukon and hustled to the rear of the SUV behind us. One cop stayed with us on either side of the vehicle. "Just stay put, ladies. This will be over quickly."

He was right. Andre and Andre Junior were both pulled from the car and arrested without incident. Detective Jimenez rounded the back of the SUV with a smile on his face.

"Ladies, thank god you're alright! We had just enough time to pull this together."

"How did you know what was happening?" Gemma asked.

Jimenez pointed at me. "Ask her. She's the one who tipped us off."

Ashleigh and Gemma both turned to me with expectant looks on their faces.

I explained what I had done. "Well, I activated the camera in Mercedes's phone charger and texted the link to Jimenez."

He continued the explanation. "When I got a text from Darcy, and it said 'open immediately 911 urgent,' I did as she asked. I also forwarded the link to Deputy Murdock. We recorded the whole thing, and the deputy got the rapid response team pulled together. Our biggest worry was not getting here in time."

Ashleigh snorted. "Good thing that light was red, I guess, huh?"

Jimenez smiled. "Yeah, well, that may have been on purpose. It wasn't going to turn green for a while."

"What happens now?" My question hung in the air, and everyone stared at Jimenez.

"Well, the Sheriff's department will charge these guys with wire fraud since the crimes were committed here. I suspect now they'll add felony menacing and kidnapping to the list as well. My office will add a few charges since the cameras were actually placed in our 'hood, and AJ tried to run you down, Darcy, so that's attempted murder. We should be able to recover most of the money, depending on how much they've spent. But from what they said, they've been hoarding it, so we should be able to get most of it back. You did good, ladies. Real good."

He walked off, and a deputy stepped over. "You want a lift back to your cars? Murdock wants you to come to the station for debriefing."

Gemma nodded. "Yeah, that would be nice, thank you."

Thirty-Four

"That's the last of it!" I chirped at the sweaty, surly man carrying the last of my possessions to the moving van. I turned around to face Ashleigh. "I can't believe I'm doing this!"

"What? Moving in with Gemma or renting your house to me?"

"Both? I never thought I'd move in with someone or be a landlord, and now I'm doing both on the same day!"

She passed me the lease, the ink from her signature still wet. "No take-backs! The papers are signed!"

I smiled and slid the stack into a folder, which went into my messenger bag. "No take-backs," I agreed.

"And you're okay with me camming from here?"

"Yep. Just please, no glitter! It's like herpes – you can never get rid of it."

She laughed for a moment, then turned serious. "Really, thanks for this. With Club Chubby closing, it was going to be back to Cali for me if I didn't find a place I could afford."

She reached out to hug me, and we squeezed each other for a moment. "I feel so much better renting to someone I know. This works out really well for me, too!"

"Have you seen Gemma's place yet? Er, your place, too, I guess?"

"No, she wouldn't let me over there. She wanted it to be a surprise." I was a little put off by that too, truth be told.

"Oh, my god! You're going to love it so much!"

"*You've* seen it? Has she let everyone see it except me?"

Ashleigh, bless her heart, had no guile. "Um, yeah, I think so. I mean, I've been there, a couple of the girls from the club have been there, even Chubby and Olenna have been there."

I bristled at this news. I had been banned from Gemma's house for the last six weeks while her remodeling plans got revamped with the reward money Tawney paid us. I took a chunk, fixed a couple of things at my place, replaced the water heater, and got it ready to rent.

When Andre and AJ got arrested, the police were able to give back most of the money to the victims. Some of it had been spent, though, and since the police couldn't tell whose money had been used, they apportioned the loss across everyone. XX Cam recovered ninety-seven percent of its money.

The arrests also exposed Little Chub's scheme to bulldoze the club and build condos. To everyone's surprise, Big Chub was supportive of the idea and even put up the extra money Gino needed to close the deal – for a cut of the revenue, of course.

Chubby, for his part, was ready to really retire and travel with Olenna. Despite her dalliances with women—which Chubby supported—their May-September romance was real, apparently, and they wanted to spend time on the road while he still had the energy to keep up with her. But even with all that, Gemma still found time on their schedule to get them over to see the home I was moving into but not allowed to see. It was very frustrating.

Well, the time was now here. My belongings were all headed for Gemma's in a cloud of diesel smoke, and I wasn't planning on being far behind them.

I held out the keys I'd had made. "Here you go, Ashleigh. The keys to the castle."

She smiled. "Thanks, *Ruby*! I'm going to go grab some stuff from my car and get started!"

As she scampered away, I laughed at her inflection of my stage name. Once we solved the mystery of the missing money, Tawney came clean and told the girls at XX Cam the truth about my identity. I expected them to be angry – after all, part of the reason for me being embedded with them was to investigate them. But they were all just so glad to have the finances straightened out, and get their pay back on track, that they either didn't think that deeply about it, or they forgave it immediately.

Amber was sad I was coming back to Colorado. She said I was her best roommate, even though I'd been there for all of a week—and that included Ashleigh, who seemed wonderful once I got to know her, which I did while we were debriefed about our sting operation and gave our depositions.

In any case, I kept my stage name and stayed in contact with the women in California. I told Luna to keep the money I was due from the videos and show I did with Reesie, but she insisted on paying me, and at the end of the month, the money hit my account.

I talked to Gemma about the possibility of continuing to work with XX Cam, hoping that she'd want to do it with me. She gave me the same speech that she had when we started—that it was an addictive lifestyle, and it was easy to get sucked into it. Still, I kept up with the messages I received from my new fans, responding to them as best I could without knowing if I would have a schedule or not.

I shook all these thoughts out of my head and walked to the door, holding it open for Ashleigh as she returned with two boxes in her arms.

"Are you leaving?"

I nodded. "Yeah, I want to get over there and see what all the fuss is about."

"Well, here," she sat the boxes down, "give me one more hug before you go. Thanks again, Ruby. Darcy. Whoever you are, thank you so much! Now go check out your new home! You're going to love it! Text me and let me know what your favorite part is!"

Thirty-Five

I pulled up to Gemma's house, and I could barely recognize the place. The front was mostly the same, except the entry seemed like it had been moved, and the two-car detached garage was now a three-car attached garage. Across the rear of the house was a rooftop that looked like it was as large as the original house.

The house originally had been a two-bedroom, two-bathroom house with a den, and Gemma bought it because the previous owners had modified it. The master bedroom had a massive bath with a shower to die for and a walk-in closet. The tradeoff was the second bedroom lost its bathroom. Since Gemma lived alone, that wasn't a problem. Then I came along.

I flipped a U-turn and parked in front. The moving van had backed into the driveway, and the three men were lowering the ramps and getting ready to ferry boxes into the house. I had put color-coded stickers on them, per Gemma's instructions. Blue for my office, green for the bedroom, orange for the kitchen, red for the garage, where all my excess stuff would go for the time being.

The movers laid down a cling-wrap style covering to protect the carpet from their shoes, and

Gemma was giving the main guy the instructions when I walked up. She ran over to me and hugged me, squealing and jumping up and down.

"Darcy! I can't believe moving day is finally here! God, it's been killing me keeping you away, but I wanted this to be a surprise."

I hugged her back and gave her a quick kiss on the lips. "I don't know how I had the self-control to stay away, but I did. Now that everyone in the city *except* for me has seen it give me the tour!"

She caught my heavily applied sarcasm and knew exactly where I'd gotten my information. "Oh Ashleigh, she has such a big mouth sometimes. Come on, Darce. Let's go!"

We walked in, and yes, the entry had been moved five feet to the right and opened directly into the family room, where before it was a short hallway with a wall on either side. Gemma started the tour.

"So you see, the entry has been moved. We shifted it over," she was walking toward the hall that led to the bedroom and office, "and added a bathroom right here!"

Gemma turned to the left. "You can see the wall here. We'll come back to this. Since we moved the entry and cut the width of the family room, and made a formal office for you, that also cut the width of the kitchen. So we added another ten feet onto the back of the house to extend the kitchen."

The kitchen was longer and narrower than it used to be. The dining area was now between the kitchen and the family room.

"Now, let's check your office!" Gemma led me to a door in the new wall, letting one of the movers' exit before we entered. The room wasn't enormous but had a closet at one end and a bathroom at the other. I was guessing that the room was ten feet by thirteen feet. Plenty of room for my desk, and maybe even a bistro table and a small couch. I shook my head. I could decorate later.

"How did you manage to fit this in? What happened to the master bedroom?"

Gemma smiled. "Come on, I'll show you."

We dodged around the moving guys again and went to what was now *our* bedroom. Gemma pointed at the wall on the left-hand side. "We took out the walk-in closet to pick up four feet of width and moved it to the extension off the back of the house, so we have more closet space now too!"

"And your office?"

"I had to give up three feet to get enough for the bathroom. But that's alright, it's still about the same size as yours."

I was about to apologize to her for making her give up office space, but she cut me off.

"And seriously, it's okay! I'd much rather have the extra bathroom! Now, let's look at the rest of the modifications."

"There's more?"

"Baby, you ain't seen nothing yet."

She took my hand and led me to my office, into the new bathroom. It had a shower, not as big as the master, but larger than the one I had in the other house. The size isn't what had my eye, though. It was the wall.

The entire back wall was frosted glass, opaque, with light coming through from the other side. "Gemma, that's amazing!"

She just smiled and flipped a wall switch. There was an audible "pop," and the opaque glass became crystal clear. I could see a massive room on the other side, but Gemma flipped the switch before I took in the details, and the wall turned opaque again.

"No, Darce, *that's* amazing. Poly-something liquid crystal glass. It turns opaque when electric current hits it."

"What was on the other side? That wasn't your yard."

"It wasn't *our* yard."

"Okay, *our* yard. What was it?"

"Well, this is the part that Tawney helped us with. Come on, I'll show you!" She led me back out of my office to the master bedroom and a door on the back wall. She paused with her hand on the knob. "Are you ready for this?"

I was getting frustrated again. "Yes, for god's sake! Open the damn door!"

She pushed the door open and held it for me as I stepped through. I stepped on a rubberized surface, as one would find at a gym. In point of fact, it's because it *was* a gym. A pair of huge LED monitors hung from the ceiling, which was at least fifteen feet high. Two treadmills were facing the monitors. The rubberized floor ran the entire width of this end of this enormous room and was about twenty feet wide. I recognized a Smith rack for doing squats, a row of dumbbells, and racks of free weights. This had everything we would need to work out.

My mouth must have been hanging open because Gemma was giddy. "I *knew* you'd love it!"

I looked down the length of the room. The center section of the ceiling was mostly glass, letting in a tremendous amount of light. Past the rubber gym surface, the flooring turned into fake grass. Not astroturf, fake *grass!* Closer to the far wall, there was an in-ground hot tub adjacent to a two-lane lap pool. Floating in the pool were two familiar faces.

Amber saw me first and started squealing. She splashed to the edge of the pool and hauled her naked body out. With one arm controlling the bounce in her breasts, she ran over to me, releasing them at the last minute and giving me an enormous hug. "Ruby! You're finally here! I've missed you!"

I looked at Gemma. "Well, you could have come over to my house. But someone had me sequestered."

Gemma looked offended, but I knew it was just an act. "I wanted the house to be a surprise. This room was all Tawney, and she insisted on secrecy."

"I wanted to surprise you, Darcy, for all your help and willingness to immerse yourself in the XX Cam lifestyle."

I hadn't seen Tawney walk up to us because I was busy being mauled by Amber. "Tawney, you didn't have to. Really, I was glad to help you and the rest of the girls."

Her pink hair was wet and hung down past her waist. Unlike Amber, she wore a bikini; but for all it covered, she may as well have been naked. I was feeling overdressed. This felt a little like the house in the Hollywood Hills.

The Argentinian beauty continued. "Well, it's not all entirely selfless. Gemma talked to me about your desire to remain with XX Cam. So, we designed this to be cam friendly." She pointed to the grass. "You can set up some outdoor shots in here, safely. Out of the prying eyes of the public. Gemma?"

I looked at Gemma, and she pressed a button on a remote. Above my head, machines whirred and groaned, and the massive glass panels began to move; first one, then the next, then the next, each one lowering on a track and sliding out of the way, like a series of sunroofs. The blue sky was clear, the sun warm on my skin. "Wow! It really does feel like the outdoors now! Though, without the risk of getting caught, it's not quite the same."

"You'll still have to do remotes and all the things like the girls in LA. But this is the main site for XX Cam, Rocky Mountains!" Tawney was beaming as I'd never seen her before. She was proud of the space she's helped to create.

"We'll have to get the camera and equipment. I can't get up and running right away."

Tawney pointed toward the far end, by the garage, which I just now noticed had an entrance to this room. In the corner, opposite the kitchen, was a set that looked like a family room with a black leather couch, table, light, beige carpet. And a large trolly on fat ten-inch wheels. "All the equipment you need is there in that rolling cabinet. And you can move it anywhere. If you want to do a show from the hot tub, you can do that. Or while you work out. Whatever you want to do!"

It was overwhelming. "I don't know what to say. This is way too much. There's no way the reward you were talking about paid for this."

She was nonchalant about the money. "It covered about half. The rest, consider it an XX Cam investment. It's like the rent on our house in the hills; it's all a capital expense and a write-off."

I looked to Gemma. "And you're okay with this? I mean, you must be because it's built, but you're okay with me camming?"

"I know you wanted to do it, and since I get to keep you here, I'm all for it. Besides," she wrapped an arm around me, "who says you're the only one who will be doing it?"

I felt a smile creep over my face. "Oh, snap. This is going to be fun!"

From The Author

I hope you enjoyed this little tale. Writing Gemma and Darcy is a lot of fun. I never thought I'd have a *second* book featuring them; after all, the first one came to me in such a unique way. But here we are. Please take the time to rate the book as that is SO important to independent authors. If you have a few more minutes, a review would be great too. No pressure, though.

Researching the cam industry was both fun and informative. I learned that successful people treat it like a job, build their community, and are sweet and gracious. But it is work and takes a toll on them, mentally and physically. If you engage in commerce with a cammer (or any sex worker), be kind, remember that they're hard-working people, and for god's sake, tip well.

Stay naughty,

HAB

About The Author

 Hi! I'm HA Blackwood. It's a pen name, but I've grown pretty fond of it. I love the people I've met undertaking this adventure in writing erotic romance. I've made a lot of friends, and we've had a lot of fun together. Don't read too much into that. Wink. I love the arid high plains desert of Colorado and enjoy exploring with the boss of me, a feisty beagle with a nose for rabbits and an insatiable love of the trail. There are more adventures planned in my little universe, some with Darcy and Gemma and some with other characters. Stick around—you'll be (hopefully) pleasantly surprised.

Other Books From H.A. Blackwood

Tell-Tale Hearts

Darcy Ford is coming off an ill-advised relationship that ended in disaster. When she's at her lowest point, she meets a woman who takes her back ten years to a night of wild passion. A night when she met-and lost-someone who opened new worlds to her. A night where her heart was stolen. A night which was the beginning of this most recent disastrous affair. Only by re-telling these tales can she find her way back to her lost love and the return of her heart.

Adored: A Collection Of Poetry

Whimsical. Fantastical. Celestial.

The poems in this book reflect a lot of different things, but they all have one thing in common: you'll wish they were written about you. You'll wish this was a permanent tribute to you, the reader, on display for the world to see.

Such is the magic of the written word. It can bring out many emotions, but the one you'll be left with after reading this book is simply this: adored.

Other Books From Baying Hound Media

Still Yours
By Cara Roman

High school sweethearts, Ridge left Leigha shortly after graduation to follow his dreams of a career in the music business. Finding his success but missing home, he is back twelve years later, trying to earn a second chance with Leigha. Ridge isn't some eighteen-year-old teenager anymore; a lot has changed. Can Leigha open up and trust her heart to the man who broke it all those years ago?

Definitely Memorable
By Cara Roman

Caitlyn has always dreamed of vacationing in Ireland. After a disappointing divorce, she decides it's time she does something for herself. What she didn't count on was meeting a charming and devastatingly handsome Irishman, Nolan, in a pub. Unable or

unwilling to deny the chemistry between them, she throws caution to the wind embarking on a whirlwind romance. Love is never as simple as it seems, though, and hers takes a course she could never have predicted.

Without A Wolf (Big Woods Pack Book One)
By Cara Roman

New in town, Emma Lowe was hiding a big secret. Wolf shifter Kian Decker needed to find out who she was and why she was so very appealing to him. Turns out Emma wasn't the only one in town with secrets. Now their lives have been turned upside down, and they need to figure where they stand.

Running From The Wolf (Big Woods Pack Book Two) By Cara Roman

The second book in the Big Woods Pack series, Kayla Decker spent years being mad at Lex Kolter. Using her anger as a shield to keep Lex at bay isn't working so well since the shake-ups in the pack. Just when they stop fighting each other new information comes to light, threatening the pack once again.